T5-ARN-338

ASSAULT!

Hawke picked up the M16 with the grenade launcher. There was no doubt what he was going to do if the powder the men were testing turned out to be cocaine.

The guard hunched over the testing box a moment longer, then looked up and grinned.

"I'd say about 98 percent pure Colombia white, the way I read it," he said.

"Where's the cash?" the bearded man asked.

Hawke sighted on the stairs and ladder of the yacht where he saw two men vanish. Five seconds later he fired. The 40 mm grenade round needed no lofting at all to zero in on the target thirty yards away.

Even before the explosion, Hawke was putting a new round in the weapon.

The high explosive round went off inside the boat somewhere with a muffled roar. Flames and smoke shot out the doorway. Somebody screamed below.

Hawke's second round hit the yacht twenty seconds later...

THE AVENGER #2

HOUSTON HELLGROUND

Also by Chet Cunningham

The Avenger

Published by
WARNER BOOKS

ATTENTION: SCHOOLS AND CORPORATIONS

WARNER books are available at quantity discounts with bulk purchase for educational, business, or sales promotional use. For information, please write to: SPECIAL SALES DEPARTMENT, WARNER BOOKS, 666 FIFTH AVENUE, NEW YORK, N.Y. 10103.

ARE THERE WARNER BOOKS YOU WANT BUT CANNOT FIND IN YOUR LOCAL STORES?

You can get any WARNER BOOKS title in print. Simply send title and retail price, plus 50c per order and 50c per copy to cover mailing and handling costs for each book desired. New York State and California residents add applicable sales tax. Enclose check or money order only, no cash please, to: WARNER BOOKS, P.O. BOX 690, NEW YORK, N.Y. 10019.

THE Avenger

#2:

Chet Cunningham

HOUSTON HELLGROUND

WARNER BOOKS

A Warner Communications Company

WARNER BOOKS EDITION

Copyright © 1988 by Chet Cunningham
All rights reserved.

Cover illustration by Greg Olanoff

Warner Books, Inc.
666 Fifth Avenue
New York, N.Y. 10103

A Warner Communications Company

Printed in the United States of America

First Printing: April, 1988

10 9 8 7 6 5 4 3 2 1

CHAPTER ONE

The first pistol round snarled past Matthew Hawke's jaw and splattered hot lead into the back of the booth. The next slug, a fraction of a second later, grazed Hawke's shoulder.

Before there was more gunfire, Hawke and the man in the booth beside him dove under the fancy restaurant table. Hawke clawed out his own .45 auto-loader as he tried to get a look at the man who had fired the handgun.

A dozen women had shrieked and screamed after the shots and now the patrons cowered in their booths, afraid to move. Percy Oberlin sprawled under the table on the floor beside Hawke.

"What the hell is going on?" Oberlin growled.

"The shooter is over there, across the next row of booths, toward the elevators," Hawke said. "You go to the left, I'll go right. I saw a blue jacket behind a snub-nosed .38. No wonder he missed. Go!"

The two men surged from under the table on all fours, came up running bent over to stay hidden behind the decorative booths of the Skyroof Restaurant, high atop the forty-second floor of the American Bank Building in Houston.

Hawke came around the last booth and immediately spotted the gunman in front of the bank of elevators, just past the hostess's desk. They had the bastard!

For a few seconds, Hawke had an open shot at the guy. He aimed at his legs and fired. The attacker moved just as Hawke squeezed the trigger and the round hit him but dug through not more than an inch of his thigh.The heavy .45 round slammed the attacker to the side, but just then he tripped the emergency switch mechanism and the elevator doors opened.

Hawke came up running. As he approached the open elevator doors he saw that there was no elevator car there!

Oberlin came from the other end of the aisle. They both stormed past the hostess who still cowered behind her fancy oak stand-up desk.

The gunman leaned out into the yawning opening, then he was gone. Damn! Now they'd have to scrape him off the bottom of the elevator machinery and somehow identify him.

Two more strides and Hawke could look into the gaping hole, which plunged straight down for forty-two stories and then six more floors into the sub-basement. What he saw defied his senses. The gunman had deliberately stepped into an emptiness of the elevator shaft.

But the medium-sized man in the blue suit seemed to hang in the air. He had grabbed one of the dozen or more inch-thick, greasy cables at the side of the void that stretched both upward and down into the darkness.

He held some kind of a clamp that had been fastened around one of the thick cables. It must have had a braking device, because the gunman slid down the cable, regulating his rate of descent.

Hawke was so surprised by the gunman's sudden step into space that he didn't even bring up the automatic pistol in his big right hand.

Oberlin stood beside Hawke, his hand on the edge of the opened door for support.

"My God! Did you see that?" Oberlin asked, the sound whistling through his teeth. "I still don't believe it."

"Believe it. We don't stand a chance now of catching him. I'll call you at home. Use your I.D. up here with the manager and put the natives at rest. I'm going to fade into the woodwork before the local Gestapo arrives."

"You do remember our Houston Police," Oberlin said with a wry smile. "Scram, I'll cover. Who in hell knew so fast that you were in town?"

"That's one of the things I want to find out," Hawke said. The restaurant manager came up quickly, scowled at them, then released a hidden switch so the elevator doors would close over the deadly open shaft. He breathed a little easier and turned to Oberlin.

"I hope you have some explanation for this. I've called the police. I assume that you'll remain here to answer their questions."

Hawke edged away, went into the restroom, and when he came out slipped in with a party of six and walked on board the first elevator heading down. It was an old-fashioned method of descent, but it suited his style.

Who had tried to gun him down?

The answer to that one was easy for Matthew Hawke, known to many now as The Avenger, the man who single-handedly took on the biggest drug operations anywhere and reduced them to smoking and melted ruins.

He had begun in San Diego when the drug mob had made turkey meat out of his wife, torturing her, breaking her spirit and her bones and slashing her flesh a thousand times to gain maximum pain, but keeping her alive for as many pain-saturated hours as possible before she at last died of shock and loss of blood.

Matthew Hawke had been a six-year veteran of the DEA, the federal Drug Enforcement Agency. He had fought drug kings and drug smugglers and wholesalers and pushers all along the U.S. southern border from San Diego to Brownsville.

But in the DEA he had to go by the rules, to obtain evidence and let the courts mete out punishment.

When they killed Connie, they freed him of all the rules. He had resigned from the DEA and now he battled the drug czars, the little drug princes and the back-lot pushers the only way they understood: a death for a death, a bullet for a bullet, a blasted car, house, cutting room or mule for every kid and adult hooked on narcotics.

He had been tabbed The Avenger by the San Diego press, as he waged unrelenting "eye-for-an-eye" open warfare on any and all drug dealers and connections and suppliers and wholesalers he could find on both sides of the U.S.–Mexican border.

Now he was wanted by police in San Diego and Mexico for murder, arson and a dozen other crimes. The DEA wanted him in the worst way to try to clear the agency's name. But he didn't have time to accommodate them. He was out drugbusting.

Now he was in Houston, Texas, where a drug mob had captured and was holding for ransom one of Hawke's former DEA co-workers and a friend from San Diego, Reno Johnson. The druggers had Reno, and Hawke was here to rescue him. As simple as that.

The druggers knew he was here. That meant Alejandro Lopez, the single biggest drugger in the Houston area, knew he was in town. Lopez was a man with a massive ego, an ambition that made him think he could control all of the

Texas drug traffic across the border. He also had more than a thousand people who worked for and with him in his widely scattered network of deceit and pain and prostitution and drug distribution, right down to the street pusher level. He was a man feared by hundreds of thousands, hated by most, and whom every law enforcement unit in Southern Texas would love to get its hands on.

Hawke had been in Houston only two hours. He arrived on a two P.M. flight from San Diego, had taken a taxi to a good hotel and registered. Then he went to the restaurant and called his friend from the Houston DEA for a quick update. They had only begun to talk when hot lead cut short their appetites.

Houston was not totally strange to Hawke. He had worked this town with his former partner, Will Halston, for six months once on a deep cover operation. He knew the seedier sides of town.

Now a vague uneasiness began to worm into his gut. Had Reno been grabbed simply as a move to get Hawke to town so he could be snuffed? Possible. The more Hawke thought about it, the more he figured that it must be true.

The only weapon Hawke had with him was his trusty .45 with the extra long clips that held fourteen rounds instead of the usual seven. He had sent it in his checked suitcase and had taken it out at the hotel where he unpacked.

The hotel, that had been the tipoff. He had used a fake name, but some smart room clerk must have kept checking a picture someone had given him. He had called someone and earned a reward. Hawke would get out of that room before nightfall. In the meantime he had a contact he wanted to catch before she started working in earnest.

Hawke caught a cab to Front Street and talked to three hookers warming up for the night's work on the sidewalk. The fourth one knew Juanita.

"Damn right, I know Juanita," a little Mexican hooker said with a grin. "She one of the good ones. But I got better action than she got." The girl laughed. "Hell, man, I know you ain't the kind of poon who has to buy it. You call Jody at this number, she can give you a number for Juanita. She got her own string of pussy now, no shit!"

A half hour, and three phone calls later, Juanita came on the line.

"Who you, honey?"

"You don't remember my voice? Two, three years ago. The Diablo case. I sprung you when your pretty little ass was heading into the chopper on a murder rap."

"Christ, Hawke! The damn big bird himself. How the fuck you doing, man?"

"When I can, when I can. I need to pick up that tab I left with you three years ago."

"So ask. I know you don't need my body."

"You know Lopez?"

"Every tit know Lopez. Got to know him to stay alive in this town. Especially now that I have my own string of birds. You know that? I moved up."

"And it costs you. Where might Al baby stash a guest who he didn't want to get away?"

"A forced house guest . . . hell. He's got a hundred places. In the Presidio if he's hot. Otherwise, might even be at that safe house on Elvira street down in the Montrose section of town. But, hey. Don't quote me. I'm no expert on big Lopez."

"Gives me a place to start. What kind of a set-up?"

"Place I'm thinking of is a four-story condo. Used to be a condo before Alejandro took it over as a flophouse for his mules. He's got hundreds of them now packing goods back and forth across the border down in Brownsville. Anyway, they stay there, all set up like a boarding house, I hear."

"Elvira, where it crosses Montrose Street?"

"You got it."

"If this works out, my thanks. But you still owe me."

"Anytime sweet thing. Anytime. Just call."

Hawke hung up and found a cab. Tomorrow first thing he had to buy some transport. Maybe a little camper van he could live in and move in.

Hawke stood at a bus stop across the street from the four-story building on Montrose and Elvira for ten minutes watching the place. Not many people went in or out. There were parking areas around back. Few cars moved. Must be a slow afternoon for the drug trade, Hawke thought. He went down the block and then crossed the street and came back. He picked the back door and found it open. Just inside a big black man twice as tall as wide blocked out the light in the hall.

"Yeah?" the block house with arms asked.

"Company," Hawke grunted and brought the .45 out of his belt. He had screwed the eight-inch silencer onto the end of the weapon and it made it look like a cannon.

"What the hell?" the black asked.

Hawke saw something strange in the black man's eyes that warned him. He surged to one side just as a baseball bat swung through the space where his head had been a fraction of a second before.

Hawke spun and found the new target. His .45 whispered its silenced message and a tall, thin white man swinging the bat went down in a heap with his right arm half torn off by the force of the big slug.

Hawke's weapon commanded the scene. "You, Boy Scout. Pick him up and get in the room, now!" The black man did as he was told. The room was an office of sorts. Hawke pulled the phone wires out of the wall then ripped the handset off the phone. As the black put the wounded man on the floor, Hawke slammed the .45 down across his thick skull, dropping him to the carpet like a sack of wet cement.

Outside Hawke locked the door and ran to the stairs and up to the second floor. Hawke edged the door open a quarter of an inch and looked inside. Midway down the hall sat a guard at a small desk. He had no weapon showing.

Hawke burst through the door with the silenced .45 in front of him at arms length.

"Don't move your hands, don't say a word, or you're a dead man!"

"Oh shit!" the guard said softly. By that time, Hawke had rushed up to him, stripped a revolver from a belt holster and jerked him to his feet. Hawke slammed him against the wall and frisked him. He was clean.

"You've got a prisoner. Where is he?"

Hawke turned the guard around and when he started to shake his head, Hawke hit him with a backhanded slap that snapped his head around.

"Christ . . ." The kid wasn't much over twenty. He started to protest, then saw the cold, deadly look in Hawke's eyes and he stopped. "Yeah, they got somebody but I don't know who the hell it is. They took him away last night. They didn't tell me where to. They don't tell me nothing."

"Thanks." Hawke clubbed him to the floor with a left cross, tied him hand and foot with nylon cord he had wrapped around his waist, put a gag in his mouth, then ran back to the stairs. There was no one on the third floor. He went up the steps to the fourth, cracked the door and peered out into the hallway. A tough-looking white man packing a pistol cautiously approached the door.

Hawke came out in a rush with his .45 up, but the guy still tried to draw. The silenced .45 spat once, then again, and the gunman jolted against the wall, then slid down it with blood oozing from holes in his chest. When he hit the floor he never moved. Dead men seldom do.

Hawke realized it was no use searching the house any longer. He descended the stairs and slipped out the back door, into the night. Hawke was glad to have confirmation that Alejandro Lopez was holding Reno Johnson hostage. Lopez must die, Hawke vowed silently, and he must suffer—like Connie suffered, like all drug addicts suffer—before being sent into the flames of hell.

CHAPTER TWO

Hawke walked down the block away from the house, and caught a taxi near the corner. During the taxi ride Hawke thought about his reasons for being in Houston. He had decided long ago that he loved his country and that he would fight for her, die for her if he had to. He would serve his country by fighting the terrible cancer that was eating at the soul of America. He would fight the drug trade, the insidious crippler and killer of so many Americans. He would fight forever those torturing murderers who killed his wife, Connie. And now he would track down and eliminate the druggers who abducted his friend Reno Johnson.

If he had to die in the process, so be it. He had fought with his life on the line dozens of times in 'Nam, and again for the DEA. Now he would do so once more, only this time he would pick his targets, pinpoint the worst of the big-time drug traffickers to attack. And he would slaughter them without a tinge of remorse. They were not men, they were animals, feeding on the lifeblood of human beings, and they deserved to die. Only then could he put a dent in the outlandish hold the drug trade had on so many Americans.

At the hotel he gave his key and a twenty-dollar bill to a bellhop to go up to his room and pack everything that wasn't owned by the hotel and put it in his bag. He'd be in the bar. The bellhop was back in ten minutes. He had checked and room 2041 was paid up for one night and he was free to leave.

Hawke went out the side door of the bar and directly into a cab. He changed cabs three times until he was sure there was no one on his tail. Then he found a cheap hotel and registered for one night.

An hour later he realized there was not a phone in his room. He went down to the street, found a phone and dialed Percy Oberlin's home.

"Percy, you make out all right at the restaurant?"

"Oh, hi. Yeah. But why didn't you tell me you were hot? When I told my boss I started to have lunch with you he blew his lid. You're a wanted man, Hondo. San Diego wants you bad."

"I cleaned up some garbage out there in the drug business and now they're taking some political heat. The guys who died had it coming. I don't have to worry about letting courts do the clean-up anymore.

"Hey, does Lopez still run things here? And is he at the same old stand?"

"Hell yes. The Presidio. Only don't try to get in there. He's got a six-block buffer zone now. Everyone inside is on his payroll."

"Right. Hey, I need Reno Johnson's phone number. I need to talk to his wife."

Percy gave it to him.

"You going to come down to the office, explain about San Diego?"

"Hell no. Your boss would have me in cuffs and custody before I could spit. I'm in town to try to get Reno free. It must be Lopez who has him, right?"

"Yeah, right."

"He might have snatched him trying to get me to come to town. If so, it worked. Only the outcome is going to be different than Al baby thinks it is."

"Good luck. We'll clean up after you. We can't seem to touch the bastard legally."

They said goodbye and hung up.

When Hawke left the phone he caught sight of a shadow darting out of the glow of the street lights lining the street. A minute later he heard footsteps behind him and knew someone was following him.

He went around the sharp corner of a brick building and waited. A minute later the guy came around in a rush and Hawke grabbed him and rammed his .45 under the guy's chin.

Only it wasn't a guy, it was a girl.

"Easy, Matthew Hawke," she said quickly. "I'm on your side."

Hawke kept his grip on her arm but pulled down the autoloader. For a moment he stared at her. She was Mexican—tall, slender, young, well-dressed and even in the dimness of the street light he could see her brown eyes and the flash of fear on her pretty Latin face.

"I don't know you," Hawke said.

"But I know you. My name is Carmelita. I work for Mrs. Reno Johnson, at her travel agency. She asked me to find you and to help you get her husband back."

"Oh." He let go of her wrist. "Sorry. But I have to be careful. I never know who's following me."

"You changed cabs four times. I'd call that careful."

"It didn't stop you from following me."

"I've had practice. I used to work with the Houston PD."

"Maybe we better talk. I work alone. I don't see how you can help me."

"I know Houston like the inside of my favorite purse. I speak Spanish and Tex-Mex that would leave your border patrol Spanish in the dust. There's a cafe down about a block."

They talked until nearly midnight over three cups of coffee and six doughnuts.

"So, am I on your team?"

"It's not a team, Carmelita. But I do need a base camp. You're it. Liaison with Mrs. Johnson. And suggestions how to stay away from the Houston PD and the Houston DEA office boys."

"I'm checked out with a .38, a .45, and an M-16."

"Guns are for big boys, not pretty ladies. What are you driving?"

"A new Datsun Z with about four hundred miles on it."

"No wonder those cab changes didn't bother you. Meet me at my hotel tomorrow at seven-thirty A.M. I want the tour."

"It's a start. Joyce said you might be a little touchy. She told me about your wife. I'm sorry."

"Thank you." He paused. "Joyce?"

"Mrs. Johnson."

"Right. See you in the morning."

They had walked back to the hotel, and her car. She slipped inside and he watched her drive away.

Yes, she would be helpful. At least she could be a tie to Mrs. Johnson. Beyond that she was just like another cop. Only she was prettier than any cop Hawke had ever seen, he thought as he went up the stairs to his second-floor room.

Matthew Hawke knew there was nothing more he could do tonight. This wasn't his home turf. Tomorrow he would know more, have some leads, have some targets. Tomorrow he would get his Scorched Drug Policy into action.

In the morning, Hawke met Carmelita at the curb in front

of the hotel as she drove up. He had on a well-worn and scarred leather jacket, a Houston Astros baseball cap and blue jeans outside half-boots.

She waved and he went around to the passenger's side and slid in.

"Food first?" she asked.

He nodded. Now, in the light of day, he had his first good look at her. Carmelita wasn't just pretty, she was beautiful, in that understated un-knowing way that was so appealing to men and yet so unthreatening to women.

Her hair came in frothy curls down both sides of her face but straight in back. Her eyes were set model-wide in her oval face and now shone with an intelligence that was more than just street smarts and college degree book learning. Her nose was small and straight over a mouth that held almost no make-up and didn't need it to show full and pert at the same time. The woman was a walking movie star and didn't know it.

"You've been a model," Hawke said.

"Yes, and some TV commercials, and a few under-five-lines in some TV-movies and a shot at the lead in a sit-com which I didn't get. Then I got real and decided I better work for a living. I wasn't making much money acting. I was staying at home with my mother who couldn't afford me, and I felt like an anchor. So I put in three years with the Houston PD."

"Thanks for the run-down. You have a piece?"

"Yes, in my purse. A nine-millimeter Beretta Parabellum with a fifteen-shot magazine. I usually need all fifteen rounds. It's one of the 92A models, a little old but I like it."

They stopped at a small restaurant and had a Texas day-starter: breakfast steak, grits, three eggs over easy, a stack of toast, butter and marmalade and a pot of coffee.

"I called a friend at DEA last night. He filled me in on what happened in San Diego. You were a one-man army down there. He said you wiped out more druggers in San Diego and Tijuana in three days than the DEA office had been able to do in ten years. He said DEA 'officially' is hunting you, but he doesn't know a man in the office who would book you."

"Good. I . . . we're . . . going to have enough to worry about with Lopez. He's still at the Presidio. Can you get me inside?"

Carmelita laughed. It made the corners of her eyes crinkle and her mouth turn up. He couldn't help but watch the beautiful smile.

"Not a chance. The only way people get in or out of there is dead." She paused and pointed her fork at him. "A few months ago my kid brother said he had a buddy whose dad worked for Alejandro. He told me as a joke that if I ever wanted to get inside the Presidio he knew the way."

"Kid talk?"

"No, not Diego. He's a little intense, not a kidder. He just graduated from high school and is drifting this summer. He probably should join the army or the Marines."

"Wouldn't hurt him any. Hey, Tex-Mex—I've forgotten. Give me some."

Carmelita grinned and rattled off a mixture of Spanish and English and some combination words and slang that left Matt shaking his head.

"I missed almost all of it. Just caught a few words."

"It's almost a third language down here. The druggers specialize in using it. They make up new words and new combos all the time. A *mujer*-med is a nurse or a woman doctor, or some woman who can patch up a knife cut or a gunshot wound. I can always translate for you."

"No dammit! I don't want you that close to the action!" Matt let out a long breath, wiped his face with his hand.

Sweat popped out on his forehead in the air-conditioned eatery. "I'm sorry." He looked away.

"I understand," Carmelita said softly. "Connie."

"Yes. Connie. I let her get too close. One beautiful, wonderful woman died because of me. There won't be a second one." He scrubbed his face again with his hands, then rubbed his eyes and looked away. The words came softly. "If I shout at you, or argue with you, or tell you to stay away from a spot, *please do as I say*."

"I will, Matthew. I understand." She pushed her plate back and stood. "Now, you said something about wanting to buy a good camper van for a base of operations. How about a clean used one where they aren't overly critical about the name the buyer uses on the motor vehicle paper?"

A half-hour later, Matt drove away from the Big Lot on one of the auto rows with a three-year-old Ford camper van that was fully equipped, tuned up, with good rubber and guaranteed. Matt chopped his asking price by two thousand, took title and paid for it in cash. He told the man that was every last dollar he owned in the world.

Matt carried fifty thousand dollars with him in cash in a tight money belt when he left San Diego. It was part of the drugger payoff money he had liberated in Tijuana and California. He decided to keep the nearly two million dollars to use as a bank roll for his fight against the drug trade. He would use their own money to bring them down. A little poetic justice. At least he wouldn't have to worry about operating cash.

Two blocks down the street he stopped for Carmelita. They sat around the little table in the van and she took out a yellow pad.

"Joyce said they called again this morning. A man with a heavy Mexican accent said Reno is still in good health. He said that can be guaranteed only for twenty-four hours.

Then Reno's genitals may be an item for negotiations. They want to trade Reno straight across for you, Matt. A one for-one trade.'' She paused. ''The only trouble with that is they want you dead, right?''

''It's a small fraternity, these druggers. They probably had some business with the guys in San Diego. Who knows?''

''We have twenty-four hours. What do you want to know about first?''

He watched her for a moment, then looked away. ''First let's talk with your brother, Diego. I want to know how to get into the Presidio when I need to.''

It took them nearly an hour to find Diego. They pulled up to a car-dismantling lot deep in the sprawling industrial area on the south side of Houston.

They drove to near the end of the lot in Hawke's van.

''I'm not sure this is where he is, but it's a good bet. He's been spending a lot of time with this bunch of kids. He doesn't call them a gang, but that's about the size of it. My one big worry is that they are into drugs. Diego has been pretty clean. Sure, he's tried some of the junk around, but he isn't a user. He told me that one night when I came down on him. Our parents are dead, so we kind of look out for each other.''

She pointed to a hole in the chain link fence. ''In there somewhere is an old bus. The kids have sort of taken it over.''

She touched his arm. ''Oh, his name is Salazar, Diego Salazar.'' She hesitated. ''I'd go with you . . .'' She lifted both her hands. ''But Diego said it was off limits to broads.'' She grinned.

Matt went through the hole and past a rickety second wooden fence. He looked around inside before showing himself. The old bus was less than twenty feet away and he heard laughter from inside. Two youths sat outside talking. Both had sticks about four feet long and an inch thick.

Guards.

Matt walked out casually but straight for the bus. The two youths came alert at once, jumped to their feet and held their sticks. Both boys were teens and about six feet tall, but slender.

"Where you think you go, Man?"

Matt stopped ten feet from them. "I usually go anywhere I damn well please. Are you here to stop me?"

The one who had spoken nodded and jumped forward, holding the stick like a staff ready to do battle.

Matt walked closer and before the youth could attack, Hawke lashed out with a *mawashi-seashi-geri*. The sudden roundhouse kick with the top of Hawke's foot struck the staff the youth held, broke it in half and slammed both halves out of his hands.

Matt came down balanced and put his hands on his hips.

"Now, unless you need some more encouragement, I'd like you to tell Diego Salazar that I'd like him to come out for a talk."

The Mexican kid ran into the bus and a moment later came back. There were six of them and each carried a knife or a three-foot length of bicycle chain. The tallest of the six wore a T-shirt with a snorting bull on it. TOROS had been handprinted under it with a felt pen.

He swung the chain and the six circled Matt. The others looked at the tallest youth.

"Nobody talks to nobody in the Toros unless we say so. And we don't say so, you Northern gringo son-of-a-bitch!"

The six began to move in on Hawke slowly, yet with deadly intent.

CHAPTER THREE

Hawke watched the six Mexican youths closing in on him with their chains and knives.

"Look, assholes. I don't have time for this. I can't spend all day babysitting little kids. Put your toys down and bring out Diego. I just want to talk with him. His sister sent me."

"Bastard!" the leader screamed, and charged.

Hawke waited until the tall kid swung the bicycle chain, then he dodged it and threw up a straight *mae-geri*. The front kick sent Hawke's boot slamming into the leader's wrist, snapped both bones and he bellowed in rage.

All in the same motion Hawke spun on his left foot and did a spinning back-kick that caught the screaming leader in the kidney and dumped him into the dirt.

The other five gang members stopped and stared at their top man.

"Who wants to be next?" Hawke asked softly. The five gang members backed away, then hurried into the old bus.

One of them stopped and helped the leader to stand and took him in the old rig.

Hawke waited thirty seconds, then a kid came out who looked young for eighteen. He hooked his thumbs in his jeans belt and stared at Hawke.

"I'm Diego Salazar," he said.

"My name is Hawke. Your sister sent me to see you. I'm trying to find a friend and you can help me."

"Why should I do that? You just hurt a friend of mine."

"I warned him. I told him to stop. He asked for what he got, and he was lucky to have only a broken wrist."

Diego stared at him. The kid was slight, maybe five-eight, lighter-skinned than his sister, and wore a pencil-thin moustache. He had on a Toro T-shirt.

At last Diego nodded. "Yeah. You told him to back off. Right. You knew you could take him, take all of them. You didn't kill him and you could have. Okay up to there. But I don't see how I can help you."

"First, I don't deal with druggers. You doing pot, coke? Anything?"

"No. I tried it. Makes me crazy. Besides, I can't afford it."

"Good. My problem is I need to get into the Presidio. Carmelita said you know a way inside."

"She said . . ." his flare of anger faded. "You must be a good friend." He shrugged. "Yeah, I know how to get in. I went in once with a buddy just to say we did it. A guy can get killed in there. I ain't got no reason to go back."

"Not you, me. I've got a reason. Lopez is holding a friend of mine for ransom. I want him back."

Diego looked up, surprise flooding his face.

"You'd do that . . . for a friend? Christ, you'd be risking your life. People get killed in there all the time."

"Alejandro and his druggers are not people. They are

cancers on the well-being of America. The sooner we can cut them out and eliminate them, the better our whole society will be."

"Yeah . . . probably. But hell, there's so much money involved. How does a cop stay honest when some pusher offers him a thousand a week to look the other way?"

"I never said it was easy. Damn hard in fact. But drugs and drug traffic are not a part of the American Dream."

"I guess. Hell, no sweat off my balls to take you in there. As long as you're helping a friend."

"I'll let you know when. Hey, any good fishing around here?"

"Yeah. Never been, but I hear you get a boat down at the docks and go out the Houston ship channel to the gulf. Yeah! I hear there's some good fishing out there."

"In a week or so we'll go. My treat. Count on it." Hawke paused. "You . . . ah . . . you tied in tight with this Toro bunch?"

"Now and then. Hell, nothing else to do."

"Going on to school? College?"

"That costs money."

"Not much for the two-year schools." Hawke shrugged. "Well, I'll see you around. One of these days I'm going to need you."

Hawke turned and walked away, went out the hole in the fence and back to the Ford van. He sensed more than saw that the kid had followed him. Probably wanted to check out what kind of wheels he had.

"So?" Carmelita asked when he stepped inside the van.

"We talked. Seems like a good kid. The Toros don't. They could get him in bad trouble."

"I know, but what can I do? He's over eighteen."

"You have a problem. My next one is I need some illegal arms. You know of any underground arms dealer in town?"

Carmelita laughed. It turned her face into a fantasy of delight. "You kidding, newcomer? This whole state is gun-happy. Almost any gun shop has a back room or a basement with a stash of illegal playthings. Just depends how heavy you want to go."

He told her and she lifted her brows. Twenty minutes later they pulled up in front of a store that advertised that it was the home of the best gunsmith in Texas. A hand-lettered sign in the window said: "No guns for sale. Strictly Weapon Repair."

"That sign is for tourists and cops," Carmelita said. "Donnie Joe knows me from my HPD days. I'll stay in the car. First you show him five or six hundred dollars, then ask if the place is bugged. After a little paranoia, you tell him what you want."

Hawke took a roll of bills from his pocket. On the outside was a hundred-dollar bill showing. Carmelita took off the rubber band. They all were hundreds.

Carmelita whistled. "That will interest Donnie Joe."

A few moments later, inside the gun shop, Hawke felt at home. The smell of gun oil, well-used iron, and burned powder cascaded over him. There were all sorts of pistols, revolvers, and long guns on racks and shelves. Each weapon had a two-inch yellow tag attached. The man behind the small counter looked up from a work bench where he was putting together a small automatic.

"Yeah?"

"Got me a problem," Hawke said, trying to soften his harsh California accent.

"We all got problems," Donnie Joe said. He went back to work on the weapon. Donnie Joe had a few strands of hair over the top of a bald head, thick glasses, and a nose that was too big for his face and at which he swiped with his stained shirtsleeve.

"My problem involves some C-4 plastic goods. Damn! I sure as hell hope this place ain't bugged!"

Donnie Joe looked up, chuckled. "I'd've been out of business twenty years ago if I let the HPD bother me, or them tobacco and firearms people. I ain't bugged. Got me a man who comes in once a week and sweeps the place for any kind of transmitter. You're safe as a babe at her mother's tit."

Hawke pulled out his roll and turned it over and over in his hands.

"Part of my problem is damn delicate. You see, what I need is not exactly a legal purchase under Texas law."

"That is a mite of a bad scene, friend. You . . . you got any more of them hundreds under that outside one, or is that a puff roll?"

Hawke took off the rubber band and let a dozen of the hundreds fan out. Then he put the band back on them and pocketed the roll.

"Suh, I can pay for anything I need. Can you do the supply work?"

"Newfound friend, unless you want a Sherman tank, a B-17 or a One-Oh-Five howitzer, I think I can do the supply work. Let me lock the front door and we'll go explore the warehouse."

When Hawke drove away from the warehouse an hour later, he had everything he would need: eight blocks of C-4 plastic explosive, two boxes of .45 ammo, an M-16 rifle with the M-203 grenade launcher mounted below the barrel, two dozen 40 mm-rounds for the launcher (most HE but some WP), and a few gas grenades for luck. He had a thousand rounds for the M-16 loaded into twenty thirty-round magazines and the rest loose.

He had a few other bits and pieces he thought might come in handy, including a dozen of the Korean war-type pineapple hand grenades. A web belt held a variety of goodies including a garrote wire with padded handle loops on each end, a set of throwing knives, and a first-aid pouch. He was ready for battle.

Carmelita, who had stayed out of sight in the van during the buy, stared in amazement at the weapons.

"You *have* declared war on the druggers, haven't you? Do you really *need* all of this?"

"Yes and no. If I don't need it, the goods become cheap insurance. If I do they become lifesaving tools. Either way I win, the bad guys lose. Now I think it's time we find a phone so you can check in with Joyce Johnson. I need an hour or so to go over my Houston hard copy files and see how I can put some pressure on Lopez. I need to know who his number-one man is outside the Presidio. Do you know?"

Carmelita shook her head. Today she wore a form-fitting sheath dress with a high neckline. "I wasn't that heavy into the narc end of things."

They found a street phone booth and Carmelita went to phone. He dug into his files and records on Houston. There should be a handle he could twist that would set Lopez squirming. He needed a good offensive hit at the big man to let him know he was in town and ready to burn him down.

"Burn, baby, burn!" Hawke said as he read through the pages of printout. He was glad he had it set on double space. There had to be some key figures in here he could use.

When Carmelita came back he gave her three hundred dollars as expense money. "I don't want you spending any of your own money or Mrs. Johnson's. You still on salary with her from the travel agency?"

Carmelita said she was. "Joyce said she had another call from Lopez's friend. He keeps asking where Hawke is and when they can make the trade. She's stalling them the best she can."

Hawke nodded and went back to his printouts and Carmelita watched him a moment, looked at her watch, and moved to the small refrigerator. She brought out two bottles of beer and sat one beside him. Then she began making sandwiches.

For a moment, Hawke resented her care, her attention, her familiarity. Then he pushed it away. Connie was gone. He had to realize that. Carmelita was only being helpful. Besides, the sandwich looked great. He cracked the beer and took a pull. He was finding some names he wanted to check out, to be sure they were still in town and at the same dirty business. Then he would charge into action. They had used up a lot of that twenty-four-hour deadline on Reno. Was it only a bluff, or was Lopez serious about harming Reno after the deadline?

He looked up as Carmelita put a plate with a big sandwich on it in front of him. There was also potato salad and a half a dill pickle.

"Welcome to Texas, pardner," Carmelita said, and smiled.

Hawke hesitated a fraction of a second, then smiled back. It was going to be all right. Goodbye, Connie. Goodbye, sweet wife.

CHAPTER FOUR

The Presidio stood by itself at the top of a small rise in one of the many middle-class sections of Houston. It would be overstating the facts to call it a hill, but the land did slant down from it on all four sides.

At one time the original building had housed a garrison of soldiers, and the Mexicans in the area back in the late 1800s had called it the *presidio*, or place where soldiers are garrisoned.

An invisible line ran around the area in a rough square six blocks each direction from the Presidio. Not a wheel turned, not a baby cried, not a drug sale was made in that area that the Presidio did not know about and control.

There were "spotters" and "watchers" and "reporters" on every block. Every store and shop had a contact, and the big man on the hill, Alejandro Lopez, called the tune. In return there were no gangs in the area. Buildings were not covered with graffiti. No shops or stores were robbed or harassed.

While the business people and residents of the crime-free zone were protected from crime and criminals, the zone was not established for their protection. In reality the crime-free zone was for the protection of the big man on the hill. If a Houston PD patrol unit chanced through the area, spotters reported to the Presidio its exact route, where it stopped, who was talked to, and what went down.

Houston PD rarely went into the area. There were never any calls from that section, and the cops had enough to worry about in sections that had high crime rates, drug traffic, gang action and drive-by shootings.

Behind his six blocks of impenetrable protection, Lopez sat in his office on the third floor and stared out the large plate-glass window he had installed.

He was taller than most Mexicans at six feet three inches. He was forty-four, slender, in much better shape than most men his age. He worked at it by watching his diet and exercising every day. But right now he wasn't thinking about his exercise program.

Two men stood beside his big desk. One was a Mexican wearing a sport coat and flowered shirt open at the collar. The other man was white, in an expensive-looking three-piece suit. He was young, sharp and aggressive.

"Dunbar, what the hell you mean The Operation has taken over the drug sales in Bellaire?" Lopez said to the white. "That's prime turf. You and your boys get it back, any way you can. You do it today. I have another small matter to deal with." He waved his hand and they went out a door that an inside protection man opened.

Lopez nodded at the big black man who opened the door. He was an ex-tackle for the Oilers, now a comfortable two hundred and eighty-five pounds and as fast as a scat back. He was just over six feet, seven inches tall.

"Bubba. Bring in my team, I want to check the guys over."

There were four of them, the best men Lopez could pull in from his widespread business ventures. All four wore black masks that covered a three-inch slash across their faces. One man carried a Colt AR-15 Sporter rifle that looked exactly like the military M-16. The sear had been filed so it fired fully automatic. The second and third men had Ingram model 10 submachine guns chambered for 9-mm Parabellums and long magazines that extended down from the pistol grip. The magazines held forty rounds of sudden death.

The last man on the hit team was the silent man. He had a fully silenced .45 automatic, a set of throwing knives and a fighting knife with a ten-inch blade sharpened on both sides like a Bowie knife.

"Fight fire with fire, I always say," Lopez said. "If this Avenger shows up around here, we'll be ready for him. Now, to keep you sharp, we have a small mission. Hermano's boys are meeting a shipment downstream in the Houston ship channel this morning and off-loading six million in prime Colombian coke. We'll be there to relieve them of the shipment. Some men from The Operation may object."

The four men laughed along with Lopez.

"What kind of transport are we using?" one of the men asked.

"We don't want to advertise. We'll take the Buick and the Oldsmobile. Both of them can do over a hundred and twenty if they need to. Let's move."

They caravanned down the La Porte Freeway and could see the Buffalo Bayou most of the time. Down this far it was called the Houston Ship Channel and brought in oceangoing ships from the Gulf of Mexico.

"They'll be stopping at a little dock down about ten more

miles,'' Lopez advised two of the hit men with him. ''We're plenty early. We can get to the dock on an access road.'' Lopez looked at the men in the back seat. ''I scouted it out yesterday.''

The two cars took the access road, drove another mile, and then the drivers pulled to a stop in a grove of trees two hundred yards from a small dock. There was a shack and a sign that said BAIT and two well-used cars parked close by.

They waited. There were six of them including the driver of the Oldsmobile.

Twenty minutes later a thirty-foot power boat with a flying bridge came around the bend in the channel and angled toward the pier.

''This should be them,'' Lopez said. ''We wait until the transfer is made. My guess is that one of the old cars down there has an engine that's brand new.'' He motioned to the man with the AR-15. ''As soon as the car is loaded with the shit, I'll give you the word. I want you to blow out both front tires and put a dozen rounds into the radiator. They won't go ten feet without a cooling system.''

''Then?'' somebody asked.

''We move in and gun down everything that moves. By then the boat will be away and no problem.''

''There's an old guy who sells bait down there,'' one of the men wearing an Ingram said. ''I used to stop by here for bait. . . .''

''So?'' Lopez asked.

''So he's not with The Operation.''

Lopez laughed. ''Damn right he isn't. But he can talk, and he can identify people. We cut down everyone alive down there and no bullshit! Is that understood?''

The fisherman nodded. ''Yes sir!'' he said.

The power boat tied up at the dock, somebody came out

of the shack and talked to the people on board, showed an attaché case and opened it, but kept it.

"Damn smart," Lopez said. "No pay until they get the goods. If we're lucky we'll get the payoff and the coke."

One of the old cars below by the bait shack growled into life and backed down on the dock. It was the Ford station wagon. The engine sounded new, souped-up and hot.

It took them five minutes to pass cardboard boxes down from the boat to the dock and then into the station wagon. When the last box came over the side, Lopez nodded.

"Now! Hit that Ford with the rifle!"

The rifleman had been zeroed in for five minutes. He slammed a dozen rounds through the car's windshield, then six more into the radiator, then four into each front tire. Steam spurted from the radiator.

Men dove for cover. The AR-15 man stayed in position and kept firing as the rest of them jumped into the two cars and raced down to the dock.

When the firing started, the boat cut the tie downs and gunned into the channel, drifting downstream, then slamming forward and away from the action.

As the two cars careened up to the bait shack the rifleman stopped his protective cover firing.

One man lay dead on the dock. One in the driver's seat of the Ford had been splashed all over the front seat. One man behind the bait shack ran for the woods down channel. The Ingram shooter on that side sprayed lead at him until he found the range and blasted him into hell before his time.

Another man crawled out from the side of the little dock with his hands over his head. He already had a bloody shoulder and arm.

Lopez motioned for the men to hold fire. He walked up to the man and slapped him hard in the face. The man stumbled, caught his balance and screamed in pain.

''Who do you work for?'' Lopez demanded.

''Hellinger in Dallas.''

''Liar!'' Lopez screeched. He slapped him again and repeated the question.

The answer came softly, a look of resignation and death in the man's eyes. ''Hermano,'' he said.

Lopez lifted his .45 and shot the man twice in the face. Then, as the man lay half dead on the ground, Lopez walked up and shot him four more times in the heart.

''Nobody in the bait shack,'' one of the men called. ''I'd say we have the area cleared of opposition.''

''Damn, they sent the old black guy home,'' the Ingram shooter said.

They backed the Oldsmobile down to the front of the ruined Ford and reloaded the boxes of cocaine.

''Worth six million on the street!'' Lopez said. ''That is if there is really six hundred pounds here. Let's move it before somebody gets curious!''

Two minutes later they piled into the two cars and swept away. Behind them lay four bodies. The newspapers would have a field day. Lopez didn't give a damn. He had just made himself a cool three million bucks for one morning's work! He could afford to cut the price a little for everything he sent out of state.

Lopez laughed as he led the team back into Houston. They drove carefully, just under the speed limit, making absolutely legal stops and turns. This was no time to be pulled over for a traffic violation.

Behind them at the water's edge, a pair of large brown eyes watched the two cars pull onto the access road. Ben sighed. He would have to talk to the police. Talk to lots of police for a long time he figured. He knew it meant trouble as soon as those two cars pulled in that morning. He didn't want any more trouble.

The big shot types had said they had to use his dock for a while.

"Better you take a pole up the channel a ways and catch yourself some catfish," the large man who seemed to be in charge said. The man gave him fifty dollars, and Ben took it.

"I ain't never seen you, and I don't remember what you look like, or what you do," Ben said. The big man laughed, gave Ben another fifty and Ben took his pole, his can of night crawlers and lit out for the patch of brush up the channel toward Houston. There was a place there he could be out of sight and still see what happened back at his shack.

Now he walked slowly up to the shack and scowled at his broken-out window. He looked at the big man who had given him the hundred dollars. Would it be right to check the man's billfold, even though he was dead?

Ben decided it would be. That dead honkey couldn't use the cash no more, he thought. Ben took out over five hundred dollars from the wallet, then put the leather folder back in the big man's pocket. He slid the bills in a coffee can and buried it near the backside of the shack. Then he pulled out his bicycle from where he had put it that morning.

He had to notify the police about the killings. It was two miles down the access road to the nearest telephone. Maybe they wouldn't be so hard on him this time. Hell, he thought, he hadn't done nothing. He didn't even have a gun.

Back in Houston, Lopez drove straight to the Presidio and put the two cars in the big basement garage. He left one of his lieutenants in charge of the goods. They would be put into the normal distribution system.

Lopez had been interested in watching his strike team at

work. They would do nicely. As soon as he found out anything about this Avenger, this Matthew Hawke, he would find the man and kill him. Houston would not become another San Diego or Tijuana!

Reno Johnson should have done it. Grabbing the DEA man had brought Hawke to Houston. That much had worked. But where was Hawke? Why hadn't he tried to crash into the Presidio the way he attacked Ramon in Tijuana? Had he changed his operational tactics? Not likely.

Lopez went down the hall and to the second floor where his guest was quartered. A guard on the door let him inside. There was a guard in the room as well. Reno sat in a heavy wooden chair. His feet were tied to the legs, and his torso and arms bound to the back of the chair.

Lopez slapped him gently.

"Where is this good friend of yours, Reno? You said he would come flying to rescue you."

"He'll be here, and you'll regret it, Lopez."

The drug boss slapped Reno viciously this time, bringing a spot of blood to Reno's mouth.

"That's Mr. Lopez to you, bastard!" He motioned to the inside guard. "Strip the belt buckle off him. I'll send that to his wife as a gentle reminder. Next comes a finger. Tonight make sure that this pig stays in his chair. We'll see how he likes to sleep sitting up. And if he wants to take a piss, he pisses in his pants!"

The guard nodded, pulled Reno's belt off and cut the buckle from the three inch leather band. The buckle had the DEA letters and crest on it in a complicated pattern.

Lopez pointed to the guard. "Tell Mrs. Johnson that we know Hawke is in Houston. We want him here in the Presidio within the next twelve hours, or we'll ship her Reno's balls, one at a time!"

The door closed and Reno Johnson stared at it in anger and

desperation. Had he seen his wife for the last time? Was this the way fifteen years of service to his country was going to end? He shook his head. *No*! Hawke would come. The man would find a way. They had worked together for six months and had been good friends. Hawke would come, Reno was sure of it. But would he be alive or dead by the time Hawke got to him? Reno shook his head. He couldn't think that way. Tomorrow. Tomorrow would be better. Maybe then he could lie down. Things had to get better tomorrow.

CHAPTER FIVE

Inside the Ford camper van parked on a Houston street, The Avenger picked out the third name for his list. He had some shots at Lopez's operation, but he still didn't have a high captain in the outfit he could nail.

Carmelita worked over a Houston phone book checking names he had given her.

"This address is out of date on The Vet. You know him? A real wild one. Let me call HPD and get a better address. I still have a lot of contacts down there. There's a phone just down the block."

When she came back she had a new address for him. Hawke took it and waved a hundred dollar bill at her. "Work time for me. Time for you to go buy yourself a new dress or something. See you back here about four or five this afternoon."

"I could help. I can use my .38."

"I'm the one Lopez wants. You're not getting into any firefights, so forget it. I told you why. Now enjoy yourself."

She frowned for a moment, then picked up her purse. "If you say so, but I don't like it." She reached over and kissed him on the cheek.

"Oh . . . I . . . just a habit I got into, kissing people goodbye." She grinned. "At least you didn't shrink back in horror." Her smile faded. "You be careful. I don't have so many friends I can afford to lose one." Then she was out the door, closed it, and walked away.

Hawke watched her. She moved neatly, efficiently, like a dancer. She must have studied dancing. He'd ask her. He lifted his brows. Yes, she was a beautiful woman. Yes, he enjoyed having her around.

He broke the mood, went to the rear of the van, and reached into a cabinet. He took out his big .45 auto and screwed the heavy silencer securely on to the barrel. The autoloader went on a holster that rode high on his hip in special leather. It let him conceal the cannon under a sport shirt.

The Vet lived in a twelve-room house in the Riverside Terrace section of Houston, a few miles south of the downtown area. If the big motor home wasn't parked in the drive behind the gate, the man was gone.

The motor home had a lift gate and had been The Vet's rolling home for years. With his new prosperity he had taken roots. If the rig wasn't there, Hawke would try Sherman Park, near the downtown section. Old habits were hard to break, and The Vet used to spend a lot of time at the park.

As he drove, Hawke remembered The Vet from his time before in Houston. Hawke never knew his real name. He came out of 'Nam like so many others, bitter, angry, let down, feeling that he had fought for his country, seen his buddies bloodied and blown in half, while his countrymen demonstrated against the war and spit on veterans who came back. The Vet had more reason to complain than most—he had lost both legs and nearly his life in the Tet offensive. Now he spent his days in a motorized wheelchair and his specially made mobile home.

The years didn't take away any of The Vet's anger or pain. He had come from a poor section of Houston and quickly aligned himself with a small-time drug pusher. The Vet was a perfect front, and for years he pushed pot, horse, pills, anything anyone wanted, then moved up to become a dealer himself.

Now he had so much insulation between him and his actual pushers that it was almost impossible to nail him on any kind of drug charges.

The Avenger didn't have to worry about legal niceties. You see a mad dog, you kill it; you find a cancer, you cut it out. Simple, quick, effective. Just as pragmatic as hell.

Hawke saw at once that the big motor home wasn't in the drive at The Vet's address. He headed uptown to the park to see if he could spot the bastard.

A half-hour later, Hawke pulled into a parking spot a dozen slots down from the big motor home. It was under the same tree in the same parking lot The Vet had been using two years ago. He must have a lease on the space.

On the far side of the motor home there was an awning swung out and The Vet was holding court on the lawn in his big chair. The Vet was white, and had two big, tough-looking men standing beside him. Both were white as well, but most of the others around them were Mexican and young blacks. Usually Hawke would call the Mexicans Chicano, but that was a California word that had little meaning with the Tex-Mex population.

He watched the gathering for ten minutes. It seemed as if The Vet was holding some kind of audience. Now and then a Latin man or woman would wander up and talk to him. A half dozen teenage boys, mostly Mexican, sat on the grass around his motorized wheelchair.

At last Hawke saw the attraction. The big man was passing out home-rolled cigarettes to the kids. Reefer, Mary Jane, pot. A great way to hook the kids and build up his customer list.

Hawke watched, but he saw no money change hands. Only the two big men behind The Vet's chair seemed to be with him. The rest were hangers-on, hoping to get some handout.

Hawke walked closer and sat on the grass, staring the other way. He could hear about half of the talk now.

The Vet was telling war stories. In each one The Vet seemed to come out as a hero. Compensation. At least that didn't hurt a thing. A tall, slender white man appeared at the edge of the crowd of about thirty people. He held another man, a smaller Mexican. He had the man's arm twisted upward behind his back.

The Vet saw the pair. He nodded toward the motor home and the tall white man and his hostage moved that way.

"Hey, my friends," The Vet said. "That's all the time I got today. Got to do some business. See you here tomorrow." He reached in a bag at the side of his wheel chair and grabbed something. He threw the items on the ground in front of him. They looked like silver dollars. There was a dash for the money as the Vet grinned and turned the chair toward his rig.

The silver dollars all were found, and the group melted away into the trees and grass of the park. Some went to cars, others lit up home-rolled smokes and laughed a lot.

Hawke lay down on his stomach on the grass, pretending to sleep, but keeping his eyes on the motor home. The man and his hostage slipped in the door, then The Vet powered his wheel chair up to the ramp and worked a radio door-closer type electronic box and the lift moved him up to the level of the motor home. A moment later he was inside and the door closed.

Hawke waited. Five minutes later the motor home engine kicked into life, and the rig backed out and drove away. Hawke got up slowly, looking around. Had they taken the hostage away?

Not likely. On the far side of where the motor home had parked, Hawke saw a form lying on the paving. He ran to the man. It was the small Mexican who had been forced inside. He looked up at Hawke, then groaned and died.

Hawke ran for his camper. The Vet's big rig had to back up twice to get around a tight corner, allowing Hawke to catch up with it. Hawke held back, letting three or four cars act as a buffer between his van and the big rig. Hawke was having no trouble tailing it.

The motor home worked out of the heavier populated sections and stopped at a small shopping center. One of the big guards went into a store. Hawke sprinted up behind the rig, got to the door and tried the handle. It was unlocked. He jerked it open, stepped inside and locked it behind him. He saw no one at first, then saw the second big man lift himself up from a couch along a wall and fumble for a weapon.

Hawke had his .45 out and pressed it against the man's head.

"Don't try it!" Hawke hissed. "Where's The Vet?"

The big man pointed a thumb at a door just behind him. "He's got company. Two bimbos."

"Tough." Hawke slammed the .45 down on the man's head and he sagged back on the couch.

Hawke touched the door handle to the back room. Locked. He stepped back, aimed his boot at the door just beside the handle and kicked hard. The door popped open.

"What the fuck?"

It was a bedroom with a king-sized bed taking up most of the room. The Vet was naked on the bed, his stumps purple on the tips.

One girl was bare, the other slipping out of her bra.

"You're a dead man!" The Vet roared.

"So is the Mexican you left in the parking lot. You have some kind of an explanation?"

"Hell no. I don't need none. The fucker owed me money, four thousand. He never paid me. A month he owed me. Today he paid with blood."

"And you think that's fair?"

"Fucking right. He shit on me, so I shit on him. What's your bitch?"

"Another thing that's fair," Hawke said, lifting the big .45.

"What you doin'? Hey, I seen you before."

"Yeah, I was in 'Nam. You knew everyone in 'Nam. Big hero you were."

"Damn right! No, not 'Nam. Right here in Houston. You was a cop. A damn DEA cop who tried to bust me."

"Right, and we couldn't get enough evidence. But I don't play by those rules anymore, scumbag. I go by my own. You see I know you and your goons killed that man back there in the park. I know. I pass sentence. I carry out the execution."

"What the fuck you talking about?"

"An eye for an eye. You killed, so you have to die. Simple. Ladies. Get your clothes on unless you want to be in the parking lot bare-ass naked!"

They shivered, grabbed for clothes and wiggled into them.

"Man, you got to be jiving my ass, right?" The Vet asked.

"Not a chance."

The Vet grinned. Hawke turned instinctively, his finger squeezing the trigger before he was completely around. The silenced .45 went off just as he finished his turn. The big guard outside the door had regained consciousness and was about to use his .357 magnum.

Hawke's round took him in the chest, scratched through a lung, then smashed his spinal cord as it continued on through. He slammed out the door into the small hallway, death geeting him as he hit the floor.

Hawke's weapon swung back to cover The Vet just as the cripple grabbed a .38 from under his pillows. Hawke shot his right hand as it lifted the weapon. The Vet screamed in pain. The .45 slug, even with reduced power because of the silencer, shattered the back of The Vet's hand, smashed the gun out of his grip and tore a two-inch hole in his palm. Blood splattered his bedding and his naked form.

The blonde girl who had finished dressing fainted, slumping on the floor beside the bed. Hawke motioned to the redhead who was hooking her bra.

"Get your blouse on and get blondie out of here. You have a minute."

The Vet screamed at Hawke. "Who gives you the right to judge me?"

"Who gave you the right to kill that man in the park? Who gives you the right to hook these kids on pot and then work them up to a hundred-dollar-a-day coke habits?"

"Fuck you!"

"That won't work anymore. You're a disgrace to whatever uniform you wore in 'Nam. I'd trade your worthless life right now for any one of the twenty buddies I saw die in 'Nam. Damn you! You're trying to drag everyone else down to your level. You're one of the small cancers on the face of America that I can remove surgically with my silenced .45.

"I can at least eliminate one of the sources of dependency around one small park in Houston. Yeah, what difference will it make in the long run when real magnum-type bastards like Alejandro Lopez are still out there peddling millions of shorts of coke every minute? Not much difference.

"But it all helps, man. Every pusher I stop helps. Every asshole like you, who is hooking kids on dope who never were on it before, I can terminate. That helps."

He waved the girls out the door. The blonde had come to again. "Get out of here and forget you ever knew this guy. You have cab fare?" The redhead nodded. "Then get on the other side of town, and do it fast!"

They scurried out, stepped gingerly over the body near the bedroom door and went out the other door.

"You're filth, man. You've lived a hell of a lot too long already. You want to say a prayer to your cocaine god, or just go out screaming?"

"Bastard!" The Vet lunged for Hawke, pushed himself across the bed with his strong arms and stumps. Hawke shot him in the face and watched him slam backwards on the bed. One round was enough. The whole top of the man's head blew away and sprayed itself in bits of bone, blood and gray matter on the walls and ceiling.

Hawke moved forward, made sure nobody had come in from the outside, and ran to the door. He stepped outside, closed the door, and walked around the near end of the motor home. He saw the second bodyguard coming out of a liquor store with a sack. It was too late for a celebration and too early for a wake.

Hawke stepped into his Ford camper van and drove away. He was much more anxious to get to the second name on his list than he had been the first. With all the evidence against him, The Vet was an easy target. On the other hand Ed Grudzinski was a marginal case. Hawke had not quite believed what he suspected about Grudzinski, but he had no time to prove it two years ago when he briefly worked with Grudzinski in Houston's DEA office. By now the situation should have flowered or died.

He drove to a remembered address on the edge of the downtown area where the businesses became more personal and less high-gloss. He parked and went into a shop that announced to the world boldly that it was the Salishan Investments Corporation. Before, Hawke had figured out the only thing the Corporation invested was other people's money in Grudzinski's ventures. But the ventures were becoming more and more off the wall.

The hottest evidence Hawke had been able to gather was that Grudzinski's hidden corporation had been involved in leasing buildings that somehow touched on the cocaine trade. Just how was not clear, and whether Ed knew about the connection or not was also not proved two years ago. Hawke had been sent back to San Diego before he could get the evidence he needed.

Now it was pay-up time. No one sat at a desk inside a bank-like counter across the small office. He rang a bell and a well-dressed woman in her thirties came from a back room.

"May I help you?"

"Mr. Ed Grudzinski, please."

"I'm sorry, Mr. Grudzinski comes in only on Thursdays. Is there a message?"

"No. But you could answer a question. I had two addresses. One here and one for Ed at 15445 Townsend Avenue. Could I find him out there?"

"Oh, I don't think so. I'm not familiar with that address. As far as I know we have no other locations. That must be in error some way. Do you wish to leave a card for Mr. Grudzinski?"

"No, I'll surprise him on Thursday. Thank you."

Thursday, the weekday Ed had always taken off when he was with the DEA. Hawke thought as he he went back to his camper. So Ed *was* still with the DEA. Hawke decided to check the other address. He had it from an update Carmelita had worked out of the Houston Police Department. They said they weren't sure why the address was attached to a DEA man's file. Hawke wanted to check it out.

Houston is not a small town. It's pushing the two million mark for residents and is spread out over a lot of territory. It took Hawke forty-five minutes to drive to Townsend Avenue even after hitting a lucky freeway connection.

As he came down the street he caught the right number on the big brown building on the corner. There was no sign on the structure, but half a dozen cars were nosed in at the parking slots around it.

He drove past, parked half a block down and checked his weapons. He pushed new rounds into the .45 magazine to fill it, then rammed the magazine into the handle and made certain there was still a round in the chamber.

This was not a front-door type of call. He circled to the rear of the place and found a door off the alley. It was locked. It took him almost two minutes of concentrated work to get the lock open. He put his pics away and stepped into the coolness of the big plant.

No machinery rumbled. No assembly line rattled. At first he heard nothing. Then, as he concentrated, he caught the sound of a few low voices toward the front.

It had been a manufacturing plant of some kind. Cardboard boxes sat around haphazardly. A partition about twenty feet from the back door closed off more of the hundred-and-fifty-foot-long building.

Hawke worked through the boxes to a main door on the

left. Two truck doors stood ready to be opened near the center of the partition.

He tried the small door, found it unlocked, and turned the knob slowly and eased open the panel.

New sounds hit him: a fan, louder chatter of more than a dozen people. The soft whir of an electric forklift. Then the hard bark of an authoritarian voice.

"All right, it's lunchtime. Let's take a break."

There were more cardboard boxes here that shut out his view. Hawke moved through and around them until he came to the last of them. Just beyond he saw the thirty-foot-high ceiling, and a huge room that held little besides a row of drop lamps shining brilliantly down on a long table. At one end was a mechanical mixer of some sort, and various fifty-pound white sacks. They could have been sugar or some other human consumption goods.

Down the table he saw the scales, the boxes of plastic envelopes, and farther on down folded-up cardboard boxes of various sizes for filling.

It was a typical drug-cutting operation.

Lights snapped on to one side and about twenty workers settled down at picnic tables to eat their lunch. Most had brown bags, a few lunch pails. There was an iced tub of canned soft drinks, and a vending machine where the workers could get hot coffee, hot chocolate, and what looked like soup as well.

One man left the group and headed toward the far side where a low light showed in an office. It had at one time been glass-enclosed, but the glass had been blocked out with designer wallpaper of some sort.

The man heading for the office was Ed Grudzinski.

Hawke was disappointed. He scowled where he stood in the shadows. All the way here he had hoped that Ed had not fallen into the drug trap. Somehow a good Drug Enforcement Agent had slipped over the edge into the easy money game. And it was easy money, no one would deny that.

He'd seen men who knew nothing and had nothing become quickly rich simply by driving coke and horse from Miami to New York City for six months without getting caught. One police chief he had met became a millionaire in two years, but quickly cashed in his chips when a drug supplier thought the cop had turned on his new money machine. The chief's payoff had been six .22 long-rifle slugs that bored deeply into his brain.

Hawke knew it had to be done, despite the fact that he had liked Ed for the little time he knew him. Hawke found a passage around the side of the big room that was dark, and moved toward the set of offices. The blocked-out glass one was the nearest to Hawke. He came out of the shadows into the half light of the far-off drop floods, and walked into the office as if he belonged there.

"Hello Ed," Hawke said.

He looked up, surprised, curious. "I don't believe that I know. . . My God! Hawke!" His hand darted toward his belt.

"Don't bother, Ed. You never were a fast draw and you're already in my sights."

"God . . . Hawke!" He shook his head and slumped in the chair.

"Keep your hands on the desk, Ed. I figured you were getting dirty when I was here two years ago. I never thought of something like this. A cutting operation?"

"I can explain . . ." Ed shook his head. He was about forty, had a full head of black hair, bushy brows, a dark moustache and a constant five o'clock shadow from his ambitious beard.

"Christ, I know how that must sound."

"You still with the agency?"

"Yeah. Mona, my wife, and my two kids don't know nothing about this. It'll kill them."

"Maybe we could work out something."

Ed shook his head. "Not a chance. Mona was suspicious of the extra money. I told her some lucky investments, then that an uncle died leaving us some money. She knows something isn't quite right. But this . . . this would kill her. One of her friends was hooked on coke, got busted, and a day later drove off a cliff in her car."

"How many workers out there?"

"Twenty-one today."

"They know what they're doing?"

"About half do. They don't care, the money is good. The rest of them don't speak English."

Hawke saw a phone on the desk. "Get rid of them. Tell them your mother just died and you're closing down for today. Get them out of here. Before that, Ed, give me your piece."

Ed took a .357 magnum from the drawer, held the barrel by his thumb and finger and passed it to Hawke.

"Now the workers. Don't try to run, the world isn't big enough. Then Mona would know for sure."

The DEA agent stood, slowly shaking his head.

"Why, Ed?" Hawke said.

"The money! A guy talked to me one day over a hundred-dollar lunch. He's a lawyer, works for Lopez mostly, but has a good front. Told me my investment operation would be a natual for expansion. When he got right down to it they wanted a perfect cover for a cutting room. I move it every three months. The landlord don't know from shit what's going on.

"The money! This guy gave me a check for twenty thousand. Twenty thousand dollars, up front. He said I'd get a guarantee of ten thousand a month, plus four thousand a kilo when I cut it and packaged it. Costs me about three hundred a kilo to cut it and to pay for the people. Hawke, I made over half a million dollars last year!''

''Was it worth it, Ed?''

''Damn you!''

''Get rid of the help. Don't get fancy, Ed. Your party is over.''

Ed's shoulders sagged. He mumbled something, went out the door, and Hawke watched him as he talked to the people at the lunch table. They drifted off. Within five minutes everyone was gone. Ed checked the mixing machine and came back. Hawke stopped him outside the office.

''Hands over your head, Ed. You know the routine.''

Ed started to lift his hands, then his right came out from behind his leg and it held a gun.

''You or me, Hawke. If I kill you I'm still in business.'' He darted behind a stack of boxes and fired a shot. It missed. Hawke pulled his .45 and charged to the left to a stack of wooden crates.

Hawke put two silenced rounds through the cardboard boxes and they tumbled, exposing Ed. The Houston DEA man fired twice more, missed and laughed.

''Damn, Hawke you really thought I was going to blow you away. Hell, I'm no killer, Hawke. But I can hurt you bad. Damn bad. So you better stop me right now.'' He lifted the .38 and fired. The round just missed Hawke's right thigh.

Hawke aimed at Ed's right shoulder, missed, but hit him in the chest just below his chin. He went down. Hawke moved up slowly. Four shots from Ed's revolver so far. It could have six in it. Most cops carried six in theirs these days. He edged around the wooden box. A round slammed into the one-by-three two inches over his head.

Hawke jumped out and pumped three shots out of the

auto-loader. Two of them caught Ed as he started to lift up. They jolted him to the side and dumped him on his back on the concrete floor. The .38 skittered away out of reach.

Hawke moved up cautiously. One of the rounds had hit Ed in a lung, the other lower in his abdomen.

Ed's eyes were glassy, then cleared. He swallowed. "Hell, Hawke, let it lay the way it is. I'm dirty. I think Mona knows. The kids are young. At eighteen they know everything anyway." He coughed. "Do it, Hawke," he said. They were his last words ever spoken. His head tilted to one side and he was dead.

Hawke examined the stash. He melted down the coke, tore open half of the rest of the packages and melted it. Then he faded out of the back door of the building. He called the Houston cops from a mile away.

"Yeah, narcs. Send them quick. A DEA man busted in on a big drug-cutting room. He was melting down the goods when they came back and there was a gunfight. They all left, but I ain't seen the cop come out yet. Better rush!"

"What was that location again?"

Hawke gave it to the woman on the line. "I'll need your name and address for my files, sir. Who am I speaking with?"

Hawke hung up. He hated it when a cop went bad. Ed had turned about as far as a DEA agent can go. But maybe, just maybe, his little talk with the cops had put a different light on it. Who knows, Ed might look like a hero in this affair after all.

Hawke drove back toward his meeting spot with Carmelita. Maybe she would have some good news.

CHAPTER SIX

Carmelita showed up at the meeting spot across from the Day/Night drugstore at about two that afternoon. Hawke had been working through his Houston printouts again without coming up with a lot of help. Houston was set up on a different basis than San Diego. There was no one man in charge for Lopez. He seemed to keep tabs on everything himself.

Carmelita knocked, then opened the door and stepped inside.

"Glad to see you with no apparent wounds or scars around your head and shoulders."

Hawke grinned, happy to have her back. He was getting used to her being around. "Buy that dress?"

"No, I'm saving up for a mink coat." She laughed. "I'm joking. I wouldn't know what to do with a fur coat."

She walked over to stand beside the table. "I've been digging down at the Harris County courthouse, hunting up old land records, but they didn't tell me anything. I thought maybe some former owners of the Presidio property might be interesting. They weren't."

"I'm no closer to getting to Lopez than I was. But I'm figuring out how he functions," Hawke said.

She sat down across from him and waited until he looked up. Carmelita stared directly into his eyes and wouldn't let go.

"I thought of something that might help keep Diego on our side," Carmelita said.

"Yeah?"

"We're using up that twenty-four hours too fast. But this might help. There's a guy who's a kind of up-and-coming, home-produced rock musician. Came up locally and just landed his first record contract. The band is back in town for a concert. I went to school with his manager, and he called and said if I wanted to meet the band, to come on down."

"And we take Jimmy with us?"

"Couldn't hurt. I know he'd love to meet the band."

"Is this Bill Hellickson?"

"Yes. Now he calls himself Bill Hell of Hell On Wheels and the Driver."

"Hellickson was here two years ago, " said Hawke, "He had a rep for giving away reefers at his small concerts. Anything on him about that lately?"

"Not that has made the wire news. But anything is possible."

"Let's do it now. Can you find Diego?"

She ran to the phone down the street and came back. "He's home, he'll wait for us there. He just about flipped when I told him about the invite."

They picked up Diego in the van, drove up Louisiana Street until they found Jones Hall for the Performing Arts. The rock band was in a basement rehearsal area. Jimmy was bouncing off the sides of the camper during the drive.

"The Hell on Wheels band is really in town? Why didn't you tell me you knew somebody? Can you get me six free tickets for the concert Saturday night?"

Carmelita laughed and said she'd try. "You realize the tickets are going for thirty-five dollars a crack?" she asked.

"Sure, that's why I need them free."

When they came into the hall, the manager, a chubby young man with an extremely bad hairpiece, met them.

He hugged Carmelita, who made a funny face over his shoulder at Hawke.

"Carm, you haven't changed a bit, except you're prettier and sexier. How do you do it? Well, the boys just started their workout. We can break in when they take a breather."

Not a rehearsal, a workout, Hawke told himself. As soon as they went into the hall he understood. This group was a hybrid of all the acid rockers, punks, and heavy metal headbangers that came before them. One of the members wore a flesh-colored body suit with a jockstrap printed over his crotch. One had spiked blue hair, another had a shaved head. There were five of them, all degenerates.

They played four guitars and a huge set of drums. They ran around the stage like maniacs. They all sang. The song was a raucous lament with the main thrust seeming to be: "Sex with your sister's all right but I prefer your mother in bed."

Diego was bouncing and nodding to the beat. That's about all the music Hawke could find. No melody, no harmony, no tune, just a beat and a wham, wham, wham with the one hundred and fifty decibels pounding out of room-sized amps.

He shouted in Carmelita's ear. "All five of those jerks are hopped up on coke or something. Look at them."

"That's just a rock band," she shouted back.

But Hawke knew the signs. He was about to get them out

of there when the amps faded to quiet, and the guy in the flesh-colored suit came running over.

"Carmelita! Carm, Bozo said you'd be coming by. You went to Sam Houston High back in Seventy-Nine, right? I was a year behind you. You were a cheerleader. I was madly in love with you. Christ, you still look great!"

Carmelita laughed. "Yes, I graduated in Seventy-Nine. Hellickson! Yes, you played trumpet in the band and had a rock group that played for our all-night senior bash!"

"Old home week here," Hawke said.

"Bill, this is my friend Matt Hawke, and my kid brother, Jimmy."

Jimmy held out his hand but he was suddenly so uptight he couldn't say a word. His eyes went wide.

"You guys always get high before you perform?" Hawke asked.

"Hell, yes! It's a free country."

"Not that free."

"What are you, a cop or something?"

"Yeah, something. What are you? You still pushing pot and coke to the sub-teens the way you were two years ago?"

Bill Hell lunged at Hawke, but Hawke caught both his wrists and pushed him back.

"You aren't ready to play with the big boys yet, kid." Hawke held him and stared eyeball to eyeball with the furious rocker. "If I find out that you're pushing dope or even encouraging the kids to use it, I'll find your ass and stomp you right through the cement floor." Hawke let go of his wrists and pushed him back a step.

"Smart up a little, kid. Dope buys you jail, ruins your health, or kills you. One of the above. There is no alternative. There isn't any other payoff."

"That sucks and you're stupid!" Hellickson said. "You

get the hell out of here!'' Bill Hell screamed. His manager came running up, looking unhappy.

Bill bent and kissed Carmelita's lips in a quick surprise move. ''Baby, you don't know how to pick your friends!'' He turned and screeched a wild howl and ran back to his instrument and did a long knee slide on the slick floor.

''Let's fly!'' he screamed, and the rest of the rockers took out their instruments and got in position.

''I'm out of here,'' Hawke said. He marched for the door they had come through. Carmelita hesitated, then saw her brother still watching the rocker.

''We better go,'' Carmelita said. Diego nodded.

''Did you see that knee slide! I tried that once in the gym on the slick floor and nearly killed my knees!''

Outside in the van, Hawke had waited for them. None of them said a word for a few minutes as Hawke drove back toward Carmelita's place.

''Damn, I bet he would have given you some free tickets, Carm,'' Diego said.

''Maybe,'' she said. ''I'm just as glad you aren't going to the concert. He looked like a real grunge.''

''But you used to know him!''

''Some of the guys I knew in my high school class turned out to be killers. Two are on death row. Half a dozen others are in prison. That was then. Used to know, doesn't count. This is now.''

''Diego, I blew it in there, but the dumb rocker was on coke, and flaunting it,'' Hawke said. ''You can never trust anybody who uses dope, kid, believe me. I've known hundreds of dopers. They all will do anything, and I mean anything, to get that next fix.''

''Yeah, right,'' Diego said, not believing it. ''Hey, let me off at the next corner, the guys have a meeting.''

''The Toros?'' Carmelita asked.

"Sure, why not?"

"Diego, just . . . just be careful." She hesitated. "You thought any more about going on to school?"

"Chri . . ." he stopped. "Carm, I just got out of school. Give me a breather. You said all I had to do was graduate from high school. Hey, I've done better than about half the guys I know."

"I know, the drop out rate for Houston high schools is frightening—up to almost fifty percent. Almost sixty percent for Mexican-Americans."

"Hey, I'm not stuck up, I can work with my hands," Diego said.

"I can too, Diego. But I don't want that to be the only thing you can do. You have a good mind. I want you to use it for something better than minimum wage."

The van had stopped at the curb.

"Yeah, Carm. We'll talk about it later." He left the van without even looking at Hawke.

Hawke gunned the van on down the street and stopped at a different spot, a no-meter zone in a marginal area, in transition from old family residences to commercial.

"I didn't make any points with Diego."

"He's a good kid. He'll understand. He'll be there when we need him."

Hawke left the wheel and slumped on the chair near the small table.

"You have any lunch?" she asked.

Hawke shook his head.

"Forgot."

"You'll never grow up big and strong that way." She grinned as she brushed past him to get to the refrigerator. He reached out and stopped her.

"I'm sorry about the rock thing. Those rockers who

flaunt drugs are one of my pet hatreds, but it's not often that I get a chance to teach them a lesson."

"I understand. I didn't know Bill was so involved."

"He is." Hawke looked up at her. "Carmelita, you can cut and run from this operation anytime you want to. Go back to Mrs. Johnson and tell her you'd rather stay in the travel agency."

"I'd rather be here." She sat down beside him. "Besides, I have another job to do."

"What's that?"

She leaned in and kissed his lips, then kissed them again until she got some response from him.

"It's time for you to start realizing again that men are men and women are women, and us girls like it that way. I know, I know—you loved your wife. But she's gone now. You have to accept that and go on with your own life."

She watched him. His expression never changed.

"Matthew. I'm not very good at this. Never was. Talking is not my forte. God knows I'm not an expert on men, but it seems to me that it's past time when you need to come fully alive again. Hawke, I think it's time that we relaxed on the pull-out bed and . . . and that we made love."

She watched him again. He blinked, then stared at her, and she couldn't read his expression.

"You see, Matthew Hawke, you're a terribly attractive man, and for the past day and a half I've been with you most of the time. I'm starting to get all nervous and irritable and uptight. I need you to settle me down, too. Once or twice or whatever it takes. And right now, Matt."

She stood, took his hand, and he stood. He stretched out the full-width bed and closed the curtains on the windows, then sat down and she sat beside him.

"Carm—"

She shook her head and kissed him again. "No, Matt, the

time for talking is over.'' She began unbuttoning the fasteners down his shirt, and slowly his hands lifted and unbuttoned her sheer white blouse.

Hawke kissed her open lips and then bent and kissed her breasts through the fabric.

''Yes, Matthew, this is going to be so fine!''

It was nearly three hours later when they dressed.

Carmelita fastened the final button and stood close to Matt.

''Matthew, right now everything seems so . . . so perfect! I don't think I've ever been happier, felt more secure, more at peace with myself and with the whole world. I know we still have a big problem, but for the moment . . .''

Hawke kissed her nose and held her gently. ''I have wondered what it would be like, making love with another woman. I never even thought about it when . . . before. Then after San Diego and that room . . . it just didn't seem right. But today, this was right, and good. We can still work together, can't we?''

''Better than before. I need to slip out and call Joyce Johnson for a report. Then I'll cook us some supper, in here.'' He started to protest. ''No, no. Please, I want to. It will soothe my domestic instincts just a little.'' She smiled and went out the van door, and he watched her walk down the street. He'd never noticed before what a sexy little wiggle she had when she walked.

Carmelita was back before he had picked out a new target. Her face was worried as she sat beside him at the small table.

''Joyce got a package today by messenger. Inside it was Reno's belt buckle, the ten-year buckle she said, whatever that is. She said she's sure it's Reno's. There also was a note telling her to start expecting pieces of her husband to be delivered to her after the twenty-four hours are up.''

''Damn!'' Hawke said, pounding the table with his fist. ''I can't storm into the Presidio yet. I've got to weaken him somehow, cut down the odds against getting Reno out alive. I need some more handles that I don't have yet.''

''Handles? Like what?''

''Captains in his organization, other houses, where he goes to relax, anything where I can hurt him.''

''Other houses? I remember something from the property search I did down at the courthouse. It's in my notes somewhere.'' From a large purse she took a spiral secretary's book and flipped through the pages.

''Yes. Here it is. Under the name of Alejandro C. Lopez, he owns a ten-acre place about fifteen miles down the Ship Channel.''

Hawke sat up and his eyes glittered. ''Yes, I am interested. A place on the water would give him an easy way to off-load shipments coming in from the south, and a place for the big man to play. You have an address?''

She did.

''Good, where is your car?''

''I want to go along.''

''We talked about that. You are not one of the combat troopers. So where can I drop off that pretty little fanny of yours?''

Ten minutes later he was heading out of Houston on the Gulf Freeday. He turned on Interstate 610 to the La Porte Freeway that hugged the Houston Ship Channel. This could be the ideal spot where he could really let the big man know The Avenger was in town!

CHAPTER SEVEN

Hawke had broken out all of his hardware from its various hiding places around the camper van. The grenades were now in a box on the passenger's seat. The M-16 with the grenade launcher sat just behind the seat, within easy reaching distance but out of sight.

Even if Lopez wasn't on site, there would be guards and protection, gates, fences and probably dogs.

He found the access road about five miles out, checked the few house numbers he could see, and charged down the road. The Lopez estate was at a spot along the ship channel where it made a wide curve away from the road, and left a lot of prime land along the near side.

It was easy to find the Lopez place. It was fenced with those white wooden jobs usually associated with Kentucky bluegrass horse farms. The white fences extended all the way to the channel, and he did see a number of horses frisking around at the far end of the land.

The mansion-type house was new, and looked ultramodern. It had been set back from the road in a grove of trees that nearly obscured it. A winding, paved roadway led to the house, but first a visitor had to get past a heavy iron gate and a guardhouse just off the road. There was a convenient turnaround, and a paved parking area that would hold twenty cars, just outside the entrance and the image-setting white board fence.

Hawke drove past without a glance at the guardhouse. He saw two men through a window. Two men here, probably four or five other guards. He'd try the horse fence down a ways.

A quarter of a mile past the gentleman's ranch he found a lane leading off away from the channel. He took the track and parked five hundred feet into the road behind some trees that probably once graced a house before it had been taken down. The foundations were all that remained.

Hawke loaded up. He took the M-16 with the launcher, a shoulder bag with ten rounds, eight HE and two WP. He had a dozen extra magazines for the long chopper, his .45 with the silencer in place, and four pineapple grenades clipped to his shirt.

He hit his line of departure right on time and moved across the access roadway and into brush on the far side. There had been no development along here right up to the white painted board fence were the Lopez property started.

When he got within fifty yards of the fence he still had enough cover to stay out of sight, so he studied his target. He estimated that this piece of land was more than a thousand feet long to the channel and eight hundred feet wide. Maybe twenty acres.

The main house was screened from this angle. He saw a building at the far end of the land that could be a boathouse. Halfway up stood a newly built barn in the classic style, yet only one third the size it seemed to be. It even had a haymow door to let down.

A growling motor caught his attention and he saw an off-road trail bike jazz along a road just inside the near fence. The rider powered the bike down to the building at the water's edge, evidently made some kind of an inspection, and wheeled back to the barn.

He made a longer inspection there, maybe fed the horses as well, and came back to the grove around the main house just as darkness settled in.

There were at least two more buildings on the other side of the house, now masked by the trees. He had a glance at them as he drove past. One could be a big garage with living quarters over it. The guard force could stay there when the main house was closed. He had no idea what the other building could be. An older home on the land? Possibly.

With the darkness, he moved forward. The fence was more substantial than it looked. The white boards were thick, and just inside the wood was a series of insulated wires on collapsing poles that would probably extend high over the five-foot wooden fence.

This was not your usual "crawl through" farm fence. The extension wires were not up yet. They probably lifted automatically when it became dark enough. Even as he thought it he heard the whirring of electric motors and the fence gained in stature from five feet to eleven.

He thought of going around the fence out into the channel, but if Lopez' security man went to this trouble and expense he would also have protection along the shore, at least intrusion alarms.

Hawke looked for a chink in the armor. He hoped for a drainage ditch under the fence, but no such luck. He knew that cutting or shorting out a section would ring an alarm and bring an instant and angry reception committee.

He could go in hard all the way. Simply blow a hole through the fence with some of the C-4 he had in his bag of goodies. But he wanted to have a look around before he wasted the whole place. There were no trees growing up to the fence.

Divide and conquer!

He took a pair of heavy leather gloves from his shoulder bag and a roll of black tape. There was room to climb up the wooden fence and stand on the rails without shorting out anything.

He went up to the third board beside a solid wooden post and leaned his knees against the top wooden rail as he worked on the electric fence. The wires were eight inches apart. He touched one with his glove and felt a slight tingle.

Quickly he tore off six pieces of the black tape and pressed the end of each one on his shirt sleeve. Then he looped the first one around the bottom wire on the electric fence and pasted the end together, forming a tight bond. Gently Hawke pulled down on the tape until he had the wire stretched as low as it would go without shorting out. He attached the other end of the black tape to the top board and it held.

He did the same thing with the next wire, only hoisting this one upward until it almost touched the next one, but not quite. When it was taped in place he eyed the hole. It was barely fourteen inches wide. He slid his M-16 under the fence, lifted his pack of ammo and grenades through the hole and let it down as far as he could, then dropped it.

Next he tested the space, then gingerly pushed his right leg through until he could find a firm footing on the top rail. He relaxed a moment, then held tightly to the top of the wooden post and wiggled his head and shoulders through the slice of space between the charged wires. At last he made it, then leaned backward like a high jumper and pulled his outside leg through the hole without touching the wires. As he made the delicate move he fell toward the ground.

It meant sacrificing his body. He tried to twist as he fell the five feet, but only halfway made it, coming down on his shoulder and hand. It was enough to break the fall.

He grabbed his M-16 and the sack of goodies and jogged to the road, then set a six-minute-mile pace as he ran down the road toward the water.

The building nearest the water was a boathouse. He was about ready to pick the lock on the big door when he heard the motorcycle again. The rider revved the engine, the light came on back at the main house, and the small machine growled toward the boathouse.

Hawke had not tripped any alarms that he knew of. It could be another inspection. Or perhaps a visitor. Hawke pulled back into some brush thirty yards away. Just as he settled in, lights snapped on around the boathouse and the motorcycle skidded to a stop.

In the spill of the floods, Hawke saw the man use an automatic garage door-opener remote control device and the big front door swung up. Lights were already on inside.

The man hit the remote control device again and two powerful search lights came on, aimed out into the ship channel itself.

Visitors. Maybe the big man himself boating in for a day away. Maybe a hot load of pot coming in from Mexico. Maybe a drop off of a floater filled with a thousand pounds of cocaine, from a passing freighter moving up the ship channel to the Port of Houston.

The company man parked the bike, went inside, and turned on a TV set or a radio. The lights prevented Hawke from closer inspection of the boathouse. He had to wait.

It was exactly twenty minutes later when he heard the sound of motors, as a boat came up the ship channel from the gulf. Hawke made sure his M-16 was ready and the M-203 granade launcher was primed and an HE round loaded.

He had no idea what to expect. If it were a social call, fine. If not there were plenty of lights so he could spot any kind of transfer of coke or pot.

A few minutes later a sleek, white forty-two-footer eased off on the throttles and glided up to the dock. At the last moment the skipper reversed the engines or repositioned the thrusters, and the craft came to a stop inches from the white painted dock.

The guard Hawke had seen before was at the dock to take the lines. He tied her down fore and aft, then stood at a snappy parade rest waiting on the dock.

A woman came off first. She was blonde, big-breasted and tiny waisted, with flaring hips showing plainly in the tiny bikini she wore. She didn't even have a cover-up for the cool of the evening.

"Get below and help," she snapped. The guard jumped on board and vanished below. The girl went into the boathouse and he saw through the window that she used a telephone.

A minute later the same guard came back on deck carrying a cardboard box. He put it down on the deck and slit open the seal. A man right behind him nearly tripped over him, and swore.

"What the hell you stop for?" the second man demanded. Hawke saw now that the boatman wore seaman's clothes and a yachting cap. He had a full beard and looked about thirty.

"Boss said to test this shit before I take delivery. We use the best testing kit going. Takes about thirty seconds."

The guard picked a small wooden case from the dock and opened it on board the vessel. He pulled a plastic-wrapped package from the first box and opened it, took out a knife blade of what looked like a white powder, and put it in the testing device.

Hawke knew what the testing kits were like. He'd used them often enough. He picked up the M-16 with the grenade launcher. At thirty yards, the druggers would take plenty of shrapnel.

There was no doubt what he was going to do if the powder tested out to be cocaine.

The guard hunched over the testing box a moment longer, looked up and grinned.

"I'd say about ninety-eight percent pure Colombia white, the way I read it. Our lab will give you a better report when they get it."

"Where's the cash?" the bearded man asked.

"We get the shit all on shore, I count the boxes and weigh them, then make some more tests, and *then* you get your cash. You know the rules."

The bearded man grunted. "You going to test every box? I got damn near thirty of them down there."

"Here and there. Let's get them on the dock."

Hawke sighted in on the stairs that the two men descended. Five seconds after they went below he fired. The 40-mm grenade round needed no lofting at all to zero in on the nearby target.

Even before the explosion, Hawke was putting a new round in the weapon.

The high explosive round went off inside the boat with a muffled roar. Flames and smoke shot out the doorway. Somebody screamed below. The woman rushed to the boathouse door and looked in terror at the scene.

Hawke's second round hit the ship twenty seconds after

the first one. It exploded in the small wheel house, blowing the flying bridge into the water. A figure struggled out of the stairs that led below. His clothing was on fire.

Hawke switched to the M-16 and put a half dozen rounds into the half-dead man's chest, slamming him back into the fire below, putting an end to his suffering by killing him.

Hawke sent one more grenade round into the stricken boat. It blew a gaping hole in the near side of the ship and at once the craft began to settle in the water.

The woman by the boathouse door stared at the burning ship and screamed in anguish and terror. Hawke rushed toward her. She saw him coming and screeched and ran out the building's big front door toward the house across the broad pasture.

Hawke paused in the boathouse only long enough to look for an attaché case. He found it in back of a desk at the far side. Inside were stacks of bills, most of them hundreds. He took the briefcase and jogged toward the main house.

He figured he might as well do a complete job while he was here.

A pair of headlights blossomed in the darkness near the main house, swung around, and charged toward the burning glow of the ship.

Hawke got off the road, lay on the ground, as the car swept by without the driver seeing him. The big ex-DEA agent moved quicker then, got to the area near the main house, and saw a lone figure standing at the side door to the house.

Flood lights outlined the mansion and the other smaller building. At a hundred yards, Hawke stopped and loaded the grenade launcher. He used another HE and dropped it on the roof where it went off with a cracking roar. Hawke sent one more, smashing it into the side of the house.

His next round was a WP. It dropped shorter than the first

two, but exploded a half-dozen feet from the front of the house and sprayed the facade with thousands of globs of tenaciously burning white phosphorous.

Hawke put two more 40-mm bombs of HE into the building. It was burning furiously by now. Nothing could put it out. He picked up the attaché case and headed for the fence. This time he planted a hand grenade on the steel pole that lifted the electrified fence, pulled the safety ring and let the arming handle fly up. Then Hawke ran like hell away from the spot and dove to the ground.

Four seconds later the grenade went off, with twice its usual cracking roar because it was suspended in air. Hawke heard some shrapnel sail over his head but he was untouched.

He came to his feet running. The charged fence was down and dead. Hawke threw the money case over, leaned the M-16 against the outside of the fence, and vaulted over the wooden part.

Five minutes later he was back in his van. He drove on east along the access until he found an on-ramp and got on the La Porte Freeway that would take him back to the city.

When he got back to Houston, he drove to his usual haunts and saw a new-looking sports car across from the Day/Night drug-store. He made a U-turn and slid in behind the candy-apple-red car. Before he was completely stopped the van's door opened and Carmelita jumped in.

''I've been worried about you,'' she said.

''You should have worried about the other guys. We hit Lopez where it hurt tonight.'' He tossed the attaché case to her. ''Buy yourself that full-length mink coat. You earned it.''

She made sure the curtains were closed, then put the attaché case on the little dining table and lifted the lid.

''My god! It can't be real!'' Her eyes were open so wide they looked strange.

"About as real as anything gets. Want to count it?"

"No, that would make me terribly nervous." She picked up a packet of hundred-dollar bills. "Two hundred bills . . . that's . . . twenty thousand dollars!"

"About right."

"You . . . you took this away from Lopez tonight?"

"From some of his hired help. A boat visited the landing down by the old boathouse on the ship channel."

"You could have been killed!"

"Wasn't my turn."

"You killed somebody tonight?"

"Yes, two of them. They weren't people, they were transporting cocaine. They were expendables, blanks, pawns in the game. The one I want is Lopez, one of the knights of the board with some real power. All of the kings are in Colombia. That's where I'm going next."

She walked up to him slowly. *"If you live that is!"* She shivered and he put his arms around her. "God, but I'm frightened. I'm scared to death for you, Matthew. You can't go on this way forever!"

"True. One day I'll take a wrong step, I'll be a little slow drawing a weapon, or one of my petards will not only 'hoist' me, it'll blow my brains out."

She leaned back frowning. "How can you talk that way?"

"It comes with the territory. I was in 'Nam, did I tell you that? The Marines taught me how to kill other human beings when I was seventeen years old. I was an expert at the trade. I'm still good at the job. Now I've channeled my talents into wiping out as much of the drug traffic as I can. I promised Connie I would do that.

"When somebody gets me, the fight is over. I know it can't last forever. Actually I figured that I'd cash in my last chips when I took down Ramon in his Tijuana stronghold. I got out, so I'm still working.

"Nobody will sell me insurance. It's a day-to-day contract I have written with life. Every dawn, every day I live is one more day that I've come up a winner."

"You're not going out again tonight are you?"

"I work best at night."

"Not tonight." She kissed him. "I want to stay here tonight with you."

She did.

CHAPTER EIGHT

Carmelita lifted herself up to look out past the curtain of Hawke's camper to where she had parked her car. Suddenly self-conscious, she held the bed sheet to her chest. It was morning, the sun was out, and it was already getting warm.

"Oh, God!" She scrambled off the camper's bed and grabbed at her clothes, pulling them on swiftly.

"What's the matter?" Hawke said sitting up.

"Diego is sitting on the hood of my Z. He really looks pissed off. I . . . told him I'd probably be here if he had any problems. Damn! I wonder what's the matter."

"And you're a little embarrassed . . ."

"Yes . . . no. Damn, I guess." She pulled on a blouse without bothering with a bra. A light jacket went on over that and she looked in a small mirror. "A mess, a true mess. I look like I just shacked up."

"You did, beautifully."

She looked at him from the door. "Don't go away. I want to fix breakfast."

Hawke raised himself to watch her run up to her sports car. He got up and dressed. She was back soon, with Diego. When she saw Hawke was up, they came in.

"Tell him," Carmelita said to Diego.

He shuffled his feet, looked away, and at last mumbled something under his breath.

"Hell, no big deal. The guys got an idea how we can make some money. We buy this tourist junk and sell it to people at the fair, down at the park, even at lines of people waiting for rock concerts and movies. If you don't want me to get ahead . . ."

"How much is the investment?" Hawke asked.

"This is between my sister and me!"

"I wanted Matt's opinion. He's very good on investments and making money."

"Yeah?" Diego shoved his hands in his jeans pockets. "Okay, okay, I need two hundred. Only two hundred, and we can clear maybe two hundred each. Double our money."

"That's a sizable mark-up," Hawke said. He reached in his pocket, pulled out the small roll and took two one-hundred-dollar bills off it. He handed them to Diego.

"I owe your sister two hundred for the contact work and research she's been doing. You still owe it to her. Out of your profits."

Diego hesitated, then took the money. "Hey sis, I'll pay you back, no lie!"

He went to the door, grinned, and hurried outside. He was back in a moment.

"Sis, you driving anywhere? Could you give me a lift?"

"Sure, jump in, I'll get my purse and be right there." When Diego ran out of the camper, she turned to Hawke.

"You don't like it."

"Not a bit. Nothing legitimate makes a profit like that. Drop him off and see where he goes. Then call me at your favorite phone down there on the street, the pay phone. You know the number?''

She nodded. ''Spy on my own brother?''

''We better. He's probably going to buy pot with the money. That's enough so he could sell some. That makes him a pusher and he could get put away for at least a year. . . in prison.''

Her brows went up and she gasped. ''All right, I'll make sure where he's going.'' She opened the door. ''Thanks. What would I do without you?''

An hour later, Hawke and Carmelita watched, half a block away, as Diego and four of his buddies from the Toros came through the hole in the fence. The five young men jogged into the park a block north. Hawke moved his van up.

The boys sat on a park picnic table and waited. Thirty minutes later a van that had been in the parking lot down the way from the table, pulled up beside it. The five boys talked to the driver a moment, then got in the van, and it eased away.

Hawke followed it from well back. He had an idea the van wouldn't have far to go. It drove to a one-story house four blocks south on a quiet residential street.

''Bet you a Texas-sized steak dinner it's a drug buy,'' Hawke said. ''If each of them got two hundred that's a thousand dollars worth. The pusher wouldn't have that much with him.''

The boys got out of the van and followed an old man who walked with a cane into the side door that led into the garage.

''Stay here,'' Hawke said. ''I'll be right back.''

He eased out of the camper. He had one WP hand grenade in his pocket and his .45 under a cotton plaid shirt.

Hawke ran to the house and up to the side door. It was not locked. He listened at it but heard nothing.

He eased it open. There was no one in the garage. One door led into the house. He listened at it, then opened it slowly. Voices came from the next room. Hawke stepped into the kitchen and lifted the .45 from leather. He screwed the silencer on and moved silently toward a door that led into what he guessed would be the living room.

"My God, only that much?" a young voice asked.

Someone whistled.

"We really getting the wholesale price on this shit?" Diego asked. Hawke recognized his voice.

Hawke got to the door and looked in. The five boys sat on the carpet staring at two bricks of marijuana. They were probably kilos, two-pounders. He had no idea what the price of pot was down there right now.

The old man chuckled.

"Of course you're getting wholesale. I know good partners when I see them. I make about twenty percent on a big sale. Easier than making forty percent on twenty small sales."

Hawke stepped into the room, the big silenced .45 waving at them.

"The sale is canceled!" Hawke barked.

Diego jumped up, his face working with hatred. "Hawke! Dammit! You got no right!"

Hawke ignored him. "Give them back the cash," he ordered the old man.

"Hey, I didn't sell nothing."

"The cash, a thousand I'd guess. Now!" Hawke's dead-level tone of voice brought an instant reaction from the pusher. He reached slowly into his back pocket and took out a billfold. Gingerly he took out eight hundred dollars and gave it to the boys.

"Is that the right amount of cash?" Hawke asked the boys. Three of them nodded.

"All five of you outside and scatter," Hawke barked. "When I leave this place I don't want to see any of you but Diego. Diego, my van is a half-block south. You better see your sister."

The kids rushed out the front door.

Hawke concentrated on the man. "You just pushed your last sale of pot. Was it worth dying for?"

"Dying . . ."

"Right, in your house fire. A tough way to go, but it doesn't leave any evidence. Cloth bindings burn away . . . neat, clean. Your neighbors might not even find out you're a pusher."

"Hey, I'm not hurting them. How did I hurt you? You some kind of a nut?"

"True. A nut who thinks scumbags like you should be stomped into the dust until you vanish. I'm old-fashioned enough to think that drugs are for the stupid, the losers of the world, and for assholes like you."

The old man shook his head in disbelief.

"Where's your stash, the rest of it?"

"Upstairs."

"How much? Four, five kilos."

The older man nodded, his shoulders slumping.

"That's a start. Bring those two. You can breathe in all the pot smoke you want to as you die."

"You are kidding me, right? You came to steal my pot. Okay, okay, take it all. I don't know who the hell you're working for, but I'll find out. My side will hit your side hard."

Hawke stopped. "Your side?"

"Sure, pretend you don't know. Lopez is only one of the big guns in town. Hermano can do him a lot of damage. I guess they'll be at war until one blows the other one out of the water."

"Probably. Upstairs."

The old man was shaking as he opened the door to a spare bedroom. The pot was stacked neatly on the dresser, ten kilos, one of them broken into envelope-sized plastic for sale.

"Been doing this long?" Hawke asked.

"About a year. Since I retired. Damn, nothing else to do. Wife died. Got no hobbies."

"The house belong to you?"

"Yep! Sure does. Paid for! And paid for by the sweat of my brow. I was a machinist—still am, I guess. Worked for forty years, five days a week."

"Your pusher days are over," Hawke said. He took the pot and dumped it on the bed, then he showed the old man the WP grenade.

"Know what this is?"

"Sure, I was in the army. A grenade. WP. Hey, that's smoke, the kind that burns hell out of people."

"And houses."

"Houses? What the hell—you wouldn't?"

"Why not? Your're committing a felony. Possession for sale. That's at least five years. You want me to tie you up and leave you here and call the police?"

"God no! I'd die in jail."

"Then we burn down the place and leave enough pot so the cops can find it. That way you won't be able to collect on your fire insurance."

"No kidding."

"True, with most companies. You're committing a felony. Automatically invalidates your fire insurance coverage." Hawke pulled the pin out of the grenade but held the handle down that would set the fuse train into action.

"Even if you could collect, the cops will be looking for you because of the pot they'll find in here." Hawke went back and picked up one of the bricks of pot.

"Maybe we should go downstairs. Anything you want to get out of here before we burn her down? Once the WP starts burning, no fire department in town can douse her."

"You really going to set my home on fire? Christ! I've worked on this place for thirty years. One of my kids was born here. All the memories!"

"You should have thought of that the first time you sold some kids pot. Out!"

Hawke flipped the WP grenade into the room, saw the handle fly off and closed the door. They were half way down the steps when the small explosion shattered the thin-shelled WP grenade and spewed the burning phosphorous around the bedroom.

Hawke and the old man ran out the front door. Hawke had dumped the kilo of pot in the kitchen sink and left the water running on it.

Outside, smoke billowed out of the upstairs bedroom window which faced the street.

A neighbor ran up.

"Kenny, I called the fire department," the neighbor said. "What happened?"

The old man stood there a minute shaking his head, then collapsed on the front lawn. Hawke walked away down the block, got in the camper, nodded at Diego and Carmelita, and drove away.

A good fire company might be able to save most of the house, but the arson boys and the cops would find the pot and Kenny would be in big trouble. Hawke had lied to the old man about the insurance. Most companies would not invalidate the insurance just because a felonious operation was being conducted in the house. They would pay off on the cost of the house and contents, but not on any illegal contents. Kenny might never find that out.

Tough. Hawke had no sympathy for anyone who got involved in any way with the drug trade. They deserved whatever punishment they got. It was his purpose in life to make certain they were punished as severely as possible.

"Did you kill the old man?" Diego asked.

"No. He came out of the house with me."

"But you burned down the house."

"I started it burning. He had it coming. Now, what the hell were you doing lying to us about buying the pot?"

Carmelita began crying again.

"Carm . . ." Diego began. "Hell, I really messed up, right? I could get busted . . . or Hawke could kill me for drugging." He slammed his hand down on the little table. "The guys said it would be a snap. We'd buy the pot and package it and resell it and we could make three times what we paid. Do the whole thing in two or three days."

"Have any of them done it before?" Hawke asked.

"One guy. He knew about Kenny . . ."

"You gave your sister the money. Have you apologized to her for lying? Family should never do that to each other."

"I tried. Women, I'll never understand them."

"Good, you're starting to grow up. Few men ever understand women. Some psychologist said it was because women love too much. They let their hearts get in the way of their innate logic, their superior intelligence, and their common sense. Still, they are great to have around."

Carmelita dried her eyes, smiled at Hawke, and then turned to Diego. "True, I love you too much. I worry about you. You . . . you have to promise me you'll never do anything dumb and dangerous and illegal like that again."

Diego sighed. "Yeah, right. I promise. I knew you'd be mad. I just . . . hell, I just went along with the guys."

They rode in silence for a while. When they parked behind Carmelita's Z car, Diego had made his decision. He watched them both a minute.

"Okay, you didn't ask me, but I'm through with the Toros. I'll burn the damn T-shirt. Right now I've got to buy a newspaper. About time I looked for a job. Minimum wage probably, but not forever."

"Good start," Hawke said holding out his hand. "But be sure to save some time to go fishing."

Diego nodded to Hawke, then put his arms around his sister. "Hey, Carm, I'm sorry. I guess I made some big mistakes. And I'm not making any more. So I'll find a job and help pay the rent. See you tonight at home . . . unless I'm working." He grinned and hurried out of the van and over to a newsstand across the street.

Carmelita touched Hawke's arm. "Thanks. If it hadn't been for you I'd have let him stumble into the drug trade. I'll never be able to thank you enough."

"You made two hundred today, you could at least take me out to dinner."

They both laughed. Before they recovered, something made a hole in the front side window, shattering the glass, pulverizing it into a million granules as the glass crashed inward over the passenger's side front seat.

"Down!" Hawke bellowed.

He jumped into the driver's seat, started the van, and skidded the tires, racing away from the spot where the van had been a perfect target.

"Stay down back there!" Hawke shouted. He slammed through a yellow light that turned red, and saw a black car behind him violate the red as it chased him. Then a second black car powered around traffic and cut through the red light as well, as tires and brakes screeched.

"Hang on!" Hawke growled. "We've got two cars full of gunmen after us . . . after me, that is."

Hawke took the next corner, heading for the industrial section nearby. He wasn't sure if he could make it. The two black cars came grinding around the corner and he saw a long gun come out the passenger's side window and fire. The shooter couldn't miss at that range.

The rear glass in the van exploded inward and Hawke pumped the accelerator. He had to figure out some way to even up the odds!

CHAPTER NINE

Behind Hawke's van the black druggers' cars kept gaining on him. Hawke jerked the van into a broadside skid, came off the brake, and roared down a narrow alley. The van was not exactly a race car. He charged through two more alleys, praying that nobody ran out of a building or drove in from the other end. He watched the big heavy sedans behind him bouncing and jolting. But they followed.

"Get up here, Carmelita!" Hawke yelled.

She worked her way forward, hanging on with both hands. When she stood behind his seat he charged out of an alley and down a narrow street.

"I need a half block on them, then I'm going to get out and you drive. Bring me the M-16 and that shoulder bag of ammo on the seat."

He felt another rifle round hit the van and penetrate. It must have stopped in a sack of sugar or some cabinet. He dodged into an alley, which he thought might be blocked, but a big truck eased into a loading zone at the back of a small business firm just in time to let him slam past it.

When he reached the street, Hawke jerked the van to the right and stopped.

Carmelita handed him the bag and weapon and he shoved a magazine into the M-16 receiver, put a 40-mm round in the grenade launcher, and stepped to the door.

"Drive this thing out of here! Get out of the line of fire. I'll stop them one way or another!"

Then he jolted out the door.

Carmelita spun the tires, getting away.

Hawke took two steps to the sidewalk and flattened out on the concrete just as the first black drugger wagon raced out of the alley mouth. He wasn't ready. Damn! He could have bottled them up.

He sighted in on the first rig, tracked it for twenty feet, and fired the grenade, leading the black car a little because it was coming almost straight for him.

He saw three guns push out open windows on his side as the round shot toward the car. Before the weapons could fire, the 40-mm round hit the grille, exploded with a thundering roar, and spun the heavy car like a matchbox in a slow roll away from Hawke. It rolled four times, stopped on its top near the far curb, and then burst into flames.

Only one man struggled out of the pyre. The man's clothes were on fire. His hair flamed up like a torch. He ran a dozen feet from the burning car, stumbled and sprawled on the pavement, his lungs seared to death by the fire.

The second car slowed a moment, then dodged around the debris on the street and bore down on Hawke. He had switched to fire the M-16 and put a ten-round squirt of the 5.56 slugs through the windshield.

At once the car jolted sharply to the right, smashed across

the sidewalk, flattened a drive-up mailbox, and crashed into the brick front of a small store.

Hawke raised himself and ran down the street. A dozen curious people came out of stores, paid no attention to him, but rushed toward the wreck and the burning car.

"What the hell happened?" a man asked. "We in some kind of a damn war down here?"

Two men struggled to open sprung doors on the second big black Caddy. Both men, Mexican-Americans, came out with guns drawn. When they saw all the people watching them, they holstered their weapons and tried to help those trapped inside.

"Christsakes, call the cops and an ambulance!" one of the men screamed at the bystanders. "We've got injured men here. Ain't you ever seen a car wreck before?"

The men were demanding, angry, shocked by the deaths of six of their friends in the other car. Nobody tried to help them.

The two in the best shape walked the same direction Hawke had gone. One had a gash on his head, the other held his left arm tenderly.

"He came this way?" one asked the other quietly.

"Damn right! I eyeballed him all the way. He ducked into that first alley. He had some kind of a chopper."

"M-16, so be damn careful. He can pick us off like rats. Stay around people as long as we can." They passed a group of workers from a small shop who had come out to watch the excitement.

A moment later the two men came to the alley. It was a block long, with buildings of various lengths stretching toward the paved lane down the center. There were refuse bins, stacks of boxes, barrels, a dozen places to hide.

"Slow and easy," the taller man said. "This cat has been

in 'Nam I bet. He's an old soldier to work the way he has so far. He must have got Willy's car with a grenade."

"Hell, yes! I saw a grenade launcher under the M-16 barrel," the shorter man said.

Hawke saw them coming toward him. He could just slip out of the alley, but that would take him away from the street the van was on. He had to get back to the van. Lopez knew the make and color and license number. That was trouble.

Hawke retreated halfway down the alley. He saw the two men come into the alley mouth. He had positioned himself behind some sturdy fifty-five-gallon barrels. He had a good field of fire, but he couldn't use the M-16. He couldn't afford the noise, the attention it would bring. If they got that close it would have to be the silenced .45. He screwed the silencer on and held the deadly weapon, waiting.

The pair of drugger gunmen moved down the alley slowly, guns out, checking the hiding spots as they came. They moved like they had army experience, Hawke decided. They stayed under protection, then rushed to the next spot with cover.

He let them come. When they were thirty feet away he lifted the silent killer and waited. The larger of the two men made the next surge. He lifted from the side of a building, lunged into the alley, and charged toward a stack of lumber.

Hawke led him for a moment, tracked him, and fired twice. The .45 bucked in his hand as the noise suppressor reduced the explosion of the powder in the firing chamber to a soft cough. The drug gunman took the first round in his chest, spun around, and fell into the dirt. He lifted one hand toward his buddy, then it dropped, lifeless, to the blacktop.

For a minute nothing moved in the alley. Then the other drugger lifted up and zigzagged back down the alley and out.

Hawke jogged to the other end of the alley, went around the block. As he approached the street corner he looked to his left and saw the crowd around the two crashed cars. An ambulance whined up with its blinkers and siren on. Another police car came from a side street and turned into the area.

Hawke turned and walked away from the killing ground. He had no remorse—these men had come to kill and were killed themselves instead. It was a calculated risk and they knew the odds. They just didn't realize who they were trying to gun down.

Hawke pushed the stock and half of the M-16 into the ammo bag to conceal it. Then he covered the rest of the weapon with his arms as he carried it in front of him and walked down the street again away from the death scene.

It had to be Lopez.

His van had been compromised so he had to get rid of it.

Far off he heard more police car sirens. Another cop car flashed past on the street. He watched it but tried to look casual as he moved on up the street. Lopez probably had his license number as well. Which meant that Houston cops would have it soon. He walked another two blocks before he found the van. It was parked at the curb. The keys were gone and the door locked. He faded into the small industrial parking lot across the street and waited.

Five minutes later a red Z Datsun pulled up behind the van. Carmelita got out and began moving items from the van into her car. When she made the next trip, Hawke walked up to her car and pushed the weapons inside.

"You're thinking way ahead of me, Carmelita, thanks."

"If they spotted us that fast, Lopez must have your car made. The cops probably will soon. I took a cab over to my car."

"So we just leave the van here, we dump it. Drug money bought it, so it's no loss. We'll let the locals strip it down."

They worked for another five minutes unloading the van. They took out his clothes, the rest of the weapons and ammo, everything that could tie either of them to the rig. Then they got in the Z. "Let's make it more complicated," Hawke said.

"Leave the keys in it and let somebody steal it?"

"No, Lopez might kill some innocent people. I was going to flatten a tire, but let's just move."

They were a block up the street when a Houston Police car with siren wailing screamed to a stop behind the van. The cops came out with guns drawn and moved up on the empty rig.

"Just in time," Hawke said.

"Why don't we buy another van? Or you could stay with Diego and me."

"No!" he said it too quickly, too loud. She looked at him sharply. "That won't do. I'm not going to put you in any more danger than I already have. I wanted you entirely away from the firefights."

"I didn't get hurt. I was a cop for three years, remember? I've been shot at several times, even grazed once. Don't worry about me."

"I do," he wanted to tell her. "I'll worry about every woman I'm around from now on." But he didn't say it. Instead he seized her first idea.

"I think your plan to get another van is best. They'll be watching the hotels and motels. I really think that would be better than involving your apartment and Diego in this. It's not his fight . . . or yours."

"It's partly my fight, Hawke. Everyone has to pitch in if we want to win the battle against drugs. They are so damn insidious! They start out as a fling, a thrill, a wild time, and then the stuff enslaves you or kills you."

"Why can't everyone understand that?" Hawke said. They rode for a ways.

"Let's go buy a van. Do you have enough cash with you?"

Instead of buying one, they rented a better one that was stocked with linens and dishes. It was set up for vacations. So they decided on a week's vacation. They had to put down a thousand-dollar deposit and pay the week's rental fee in advance.

An hour in a grocery story and their new home was ready.

Carmelita called Mrs. Johnson. The woman was in hysterics. Carmelita told Hawke about it when she came back. "She opened a small package that came in the mail and found a finger. It had a ring on it, a lodge ring that Reno was proud of. It was so small it wouldn't come off. She's sure it's Reno's little finger."

"Sounds like Lopez. I still don't like the trade talk. That would be the last gasp. We're not there yet. How is she holding up?"

"Her sister is staying with her. They have a cop inside the house and unmarked car in the driveway. She'll make it. She's a tough lady."

"Good. Now, let's establish a park-and-meet spot closer to your apartment. I can light anywhere there aren't parking meters."

A half-hour later they were settled down six blocks from her place. She had telephoned and Diego was home. He hadn't had any luck looking for a job.

"I started too late in the morning. Tomorrow I'll be up at four A.M., get the first edition of the paper, and be sitting on somebody's doorstep when he opens up."

"Good, Diego. I'm proud of you." She told him the new spot for the van. "I'll see you later tonight, for sure."

She hung up and kissed Hawke softly. "Your new place is nice, but I want a long hot bath and bubbles and everything and some different clothes. I'll be here in the morning by eight. How's that?"

Hawke nodded and stared at the paper he was doodling on. He had to figure out a series of quick, sharp thrusts at Lopez to make him nervous and to weaken his defenses.

"Right, Carm, right." He stood and kissed her seriously, then let her go. "Tomorrow, and I promise you nobody is going to shoot at you."

She grinned, and hurried out the door, wondering how Diego was holding up in his new try at growing up. It was so damn hard on kids these days.

CHAPTER TEN

Alejandro Lopez swung a doubled fist at the man who stood in front of him. The smaller man took the blow on the shoulder without moving or wincing.

"Christ! Do I have to do everything myself! I send ten good boys after this shit and what happens? He kills seven of you and puts two in the hospital, for Christsakes!"

Lopez shook his head in disbelief and dove into the pool. He swam the length of the specially built "laps" pool. It was twenty-five yards long and ten feet wide. He came back with a furious crawl stroke, lifted himself from the pool smoothly, and took a towel that a bikini-clad girl handed him.

He never looked at her, but stared at the man who held his arm protectively and had a bloody scrape on his forehead.

"You telling me that he out-drove my wheelmen, then hit the lead car with a bomb, a grenade of some kind, and poof! There go five of the best guns in Houston?"

The man nodded.

"Then he hits the driver of the second rig with a spray of bullets from an army M-16 automatic rifle and that car crashes with one more man dead?"

Lopez swore again, finished drying off, and gave the towel to the girl. He kissed her chest in the cleavage between surging breasts.

"All right, it's done. Get out of here and have that arm looked at. It might be broken."

Lopez dropped on a padded lounge chair and picked up a drink that the same bikini-draped girl had fixed. It was lemonade. Lopez never smoked or drank alcohol. He was not a drug user.

He had used the same words over and over, and he believed them: "Hell, I just sell the shit, I wouldn't be caught dead using it. You know what that stuff does to you?" But, business was business. He made most of his money from selling drugs.

In the last five years he had made a clear profit of over two hundred million dollars. It all was solidly invested in the stock market and in Houston and Miami real estate, two of the most stable markets in the world, he was told.

The girl came up behind him and began massaging his shoulders.

"Yeah, Chichi, just what I need. First somebody hijacks that shipment in from Colombia and burns down my ship's channel place and now this little shit snuffs seven of my best men!"

Lopez loved exercising with and being massaged by Chichi, or one of three or four other beautiful and well-built ladies who lived at his town mansion.

As Chichi's hands worked their magic, Lopez thought about how, until this past week, everything had been moving along smoothly. A few arguments with Hermano and a hit now and then, but that just kept it realistic.

Now everything was exploding.

The damn Avenger!

Lopez had heard about him and the devastation he had left behind him in Tijuana and San Diego. That was when he had decided to cut short the career of this self-proclaimed drug fighter. Reno Johnson had been the bait and it worked. Only now the catch was turning out to be too damn costly.

He lay down on the chaise and turned on his stomach. Chichi began a simple yet effective massage on his back. Soon her hands had worked down to his buttocks.

"Not now, Chichi," he said sitting up. "I've got to decide about this damn Avenger."

Lopez had started out in Brownsville with the rest of the family. Their father had been a large, happy man who had been a small-time smuggler in Brownsville. He worked well with the Federales captain there and made a good living. He sired six sons and four daughters.

Then one day he died of lead poisoning. A U.S. border guard had ordered him to stop, but the load of marijuana on his pickup had given him a reason to make a run for it. A lucky shot aimed at his tire, slanted off the box, and slammed sideways through Pedro Lopez's head.

After the funeral, the six boys got together and tried to figure out what to do. They ranged in age from eighteen to twenty-eight. The oldest demanded that he take over and run the family business.

Arguments developed and at last the older boy, Philip, shot and killed his next oldest brother, Roberto. The death had taken place in a downtown Brownsville bar and couldn't be covered up. Philip was convicted and was still in prison serving a twenty-year term. Knowing Philip, he would not get time off for good behavior. Not a Mexican in a Texas prison.

Gradually Lopez had risen to the top as the major force in

the family smuggling operation. He moved to Houston to establish a larger market base, and built up a network of wholesalers and pushers that now numbered over a thousand.

The three other brothers concentrated on getting the drugs across the border. It was still rather easy with the marijuana. Pot is the biggest and sometimes the only cash crop for many of the dirt-poor Mexican Indians and farmers in the sparsely populated border states.

Lopez set up the system they still used. Pickup trucks are prized like gold in Mexico. The Lopez brothers would arrange to buy pot in the state of Nuevo Leon, across the Rio Grande from McAllen to Brownsville. Then the brothers would steal six or eight pickup trucks and, the same night, drive them across the border at various places.

The pickups, full of gas, would be traded for the pot, with as little cash being used as possible. The pot would be collected and driven back in one or two of the pickups. The system had worked so well it had hardly been changed at all since they began seven or eight years ago.

The coke was a tougher matter. That was a purely cash transaction. Cash was becoming a problem for Lopez again. He had too much of it. One of the bank vice presidents who had "cooperated" with him for a hundred thousand a year wanted out of the agreement. He said the feds were checking banks closer these days.

Lopez had something like ten million dollars in cash in his various stash houses and rest houses for his mules. If he deposited more than ten thousand in cash at a time, the IRS got a notification. That was not good for business.

At least he could buy coke with the cash.

Alejandro Lopez slammed his fist into the padded lounger. What in hell could he do about Matthew Hawke?

He also had to set up a "response" to what Hermano

must have done at his ship channel place. That hit had to be Hermano. He had to reply. He'd think of a way.

But Hawke? The bait would work only so far. He had to keep Reno Johnson alive or Hawke would go ape-shit. A trap for the do-gooder might be the only way. Yeah, some kind of a trap.

A price on his head might work. Any of his gunmen would work extra hard to find Hawke if it was going to be worth, say, a hundred grand! Yeah, a hundred grand for the gun that brings in Matt Hawke's head in a bucket! Damn, that was good!

He motioned, and one of his men ran out to the pool. Lopez gave the man the word on the price on Hawke's head and told him to spread the message to all of his people.

Lopez settled back on the lounge.

"Now, Chichi!" he said. She smiled and hovered over him. He unsnapped her tiny bra and let it fall away.

"Oh, yes!" he said softly.

"Right here?" she asked.

"Why the hell not?"

"You could get your bare ass sunburned."

"True. Inside. And go get that new one, Wanda. I can take care of at least two of you today."

All over the compound the men heard the news. A hundred thousand in cash to the man who gunned down Hawke. The Avenger, he called himself.

Yeah, the game had begun, Lopez thought. One of them was going to get lucky. Who would it be? Every man would be more alert now, ready with instant death in his hand.

Two hours later, Lopez had finished his shower and was dressing for dinner. He always dressed up for his evening meal, whether he ate alone or with someone. It made him feel good, the way it must have made the British feel when they dressed formally for dinner.

Tonight he ate with his playmates. Wanda was so young, so blonde, so American! Chichi was so Latin! He could never get enough of both of them. They were his one vice, but one that would not kill him, at least.

He considered Hawke again. A plan came to mind, a trap he could use against the terrorist. Lopez had no worries about defense. There was no way that the gringo could penetrate his layers and layers of protection. He might get halfway through the defenses, but by then he would be identified and turned back or cut down, depending on who talked to him.

By now there were over a hundred tried and true men who were searching for Hawke, eager to earn the hundred thousand. By midnight there would be another two hundred who knew about the blood money, and would surge around him to try to collect.

The trap. He needed one for Hermano, and one, a much more complicated and innocent-appearing one, for Hawke.

Hermano was easy. He would find some just-forming gang to be used as the bait to bring Hermano out in the open. Simple. He would send a man into the streets to search out the perfect group of street toughs to use.

Lopez relaxed over his six-course meal. The two ladies were dressed deliciously, with gowns that had necklines cut to the waist. When they moved just right, he could get an illicit and secret peek at one of their bare breasts.

Sometimes it was the little pleasures in life that made it all worthwhile.

He thought about Hawke again.

Somewhere an alarm rang. Lopez pulled a small telephone from his pocket, pushed up an antenna, and dialed three digits.

"What's the trouble?" he demanded.

As he listened the worry on his face vanished. He grunted

and pushed the aerial down. It had only been a delivery driver who forgot to stop at the second checkpoint. He had been cleared and was bringing in food for tomorrow.

Chichi put on jazz tapes and Lopez eased back in a recliner, stretched out his feet, and relaxed. His second passion was jazz. He had taken lessons on a saxophone in school. Jazz had always fascinated him. Now he invited special jazz greats to be guests in his mansion when they played Houston.

As the notes tumbled over him, he worked on his trap for Hawke. It had to be just right, innocence personified; simple, yet devastatingly effective. Hawke must die!

After a half-hour of jazz he flicked his hand and Chichi turned off the music. The three of them went to the patio that looked down over part of Houston. The lights were just coming on, and the city sparkled with brilliance.

As soon as the patio doors opened, two guards at ground level shifted their positions until they hovered in the darkness twenty feet on each side of the open area on the third floor of the mansion. They searched the terrain with night scopes. Each man had a guard dog chained to his waist. The big Doberman pinschers sat calmly at "heel" as their handlers watched for an intruder.

In front of the guards a well-manicured lawn and beautifully landscaped garden ran down the slight rise to a fence. It was a block wall fence, with the hollows in the block poured with concrete and studded with reinforcing steel. The builder had guaranteed that no ordinary vehicle could crash through the wall.

Beyond the barrier, a landscaped "park" had been created. No one played in this park, no children or dogs ran in it. It extended for half a block deep all the way around Lopez' mansion in a huge rectangle of green. The grass was tended carefully, and contained three kinds of unseen intrusion alarms. No one stepped on the grass without a light flashing in an underground control station in that half of the area. Two stations kept the entire green belt under visual and electronic surveillance twenty-four hours a day.

Beyond the green belt were normal houses, but most of those surrounding the grassy backyards were owned by longtime Lopez workers who were fiercely loyal. These were the hardcore supporters who owed their fortunes and many of them, their lives, to Lopez.

Back on the third floor of the mansion, Lopez had sent the two ladies away. He sat behind a huge teak and oak desk in his office. The whole thing was electronic. A button brought a fifty-six inch television screen into view on the near wall. Other switches and buttons controlled temperature, humidity, a sound system, intercom and alarms.

Now he worked on a yellow pad with a ballpoint pen. A dozen ideas had been noted and crossed out. At last only one phrase remained on the yellow, lined paper. It was:

"Kill Matthew Hawke!"

CHAPTER ELEVEN

Hawke watched Carmelita walk away from the new van. He couldn't afford to take the night off. He had a schedule to meet . . . death to Alejandro Lopez!

The ex-DEA agent sat at the small table in his van going over his options. One was the Paper Man. The short time he had been in Houston, he had picked up a lot of talk about the Paper Man. That was the only name most people knew him by. He sold papers from a little stand down on the corner of Preston and Main in front of the Harris County Administration building.

The Paper Man also had an ear to the ground and knew more about what was going on in Houston than all the cops on their beats. He should still be open. Hawke took the short drive, found a parking spot in the rapidly clearing streets, and caught the Paper Man before he closed.

Three teenage blacks eyed Hawke suspiciously. They evidently were at home there. Hawke ignored them, picked up a *Houston Post,* and dropped two quarters in the tray provided. The Paper Man was an elderly black man who wore dark glasses—blindman's glasses. He lifted his head, his ear slightly to the front.

"Thank you, suh," Paper Man said, with the soft honey tones of the Deep South.

"You bet, a man's got to keep up on the news."

"Southern California."

"What was that?"

"Southern Cal, you're a suntan man from Hollywood or L.A. or maybe San Diego."

"That's a sharp ear. Are you the gentleman they call the Paper Man?"

The wrinkled face relaxed a little and he nodded. "Peers as how that's me." He gave a small hand signal and the three kids moved away from them a dozen feet, but stayed alert.

"I'm a man searching for some answers. I hear you know everything that goes down on the street, in the boardrooms and in the back rooms. Is that right?"

The Paper Man grinned, then chuckled. "Say, I just want to thank you for calling me a gentleman. Ain't nobody done that in some time. No, sir. As for the other, just so much stuff and nonsense. Nobody knows all them things."

"I'm most interested in the street talk."

"There I might be able to qualify. But a man knows, don't mean a man tells. Depending on how long a man wants to stay alive and healthy enough to make a living."

"Those shades for real, blind real?"

"I got a legal ten percent in each eye. Close enough to blind. Yep, I'm betting you hail from San Diego. What kind of street jive you looking for?"

"The rough kind. The kind that tears young blacks and whites and browns apart and dumps them in the morgue. I'm looking for a stash house and a cutting parlor."

The Paper Man chuckled again and listened closely for a moment. He heard no footsteps stopping. "Laying ten to one you from San Diego and you used to be a DEA man. Yeah, I listen to the news, all damn day. News station. I heard about you. You be the man they calling the Avenger."

"I want a stash house and a cutting operation."

"Which side?"

"It doesn't matter. Lopez would be best."

"You shoot high, man!"

"I always hit what I shoot at, Paper Man."

"Good. I heard about too many of my people who get on the damn coke. Used to be horse, now it's coke. Damn! That shit kill people. You get jailed, go crazy, or get buried. My preaching don't get far."

Paper Man straightened, in a memorized pattern, the piles of newspapers and magazines in front of where he sat on a stool.

"Yeah, I got a cut house for you. Big Al runs it. He killed a friend of mine a month ago. Cut him down, no good reason. 'Bout time I do part of a payback."

He motioned Hawke closer.

"Nobody can hear us, right?" Paper Man asked.

"Not unless they have a powerful shotgun microphone."

"I'm clean with Lopez and his people. Aim to stay that way. You get out to the eight thousand block on Parna Avenue. There's a furniture store on the ground level. Around back is a stairway. The whole second floor is a cut shop."

"They work nights?"

"True. But, hey. Go soft on the workers. They just making a living. Lots don't speak English, don't even know what they do." The black face grinned. "You see, I figure you're this guy the papers and the radio is calling the

Avenger, the guy from San Diego. Whichever, you take it easy on the little people."

"Paper Man, its a contract. I see this Avenger gent, I'll pass on your message. Oh, can you change a one for me? I need some phone change."

"Proud to do so," Paper Man said with a big smile. "Mighty proud to do it . . . and to meet you. Would you . . . would you mind shaking hands with an old black fart like me?"

"Be pleased to," Hawke said, gripping the surprisingly strong black hand. Then he stripped a hundred-dollar bill off his roll and gave it to the vendor.

"You sure that's a one?"

"I'm sure."

The slender black fingers took four quarters from the tray in front of him and held them out. Hawke let them fall into his hand.

"I'll be back in a day or two. I'm still looking for a crash house, some spot where Lopez keeps his mules between runs into Mexico and to Colombia and New York. See what you can find out, but don't get in trouble."

"Trouble? Hell, that's been my first and middle name for almost sixty years now. Little more won't take the shine off my wingtips!"

Hawke laughed and walked away, the four quarters and the *Houston Post* firmly in his hand.

Parna was one of the less important arteries that angled out northeast from downtown Houston through some smaller tracts and subdivisions. Here and there a shopping center bulged out on the normally quiet street. The eight-thousand block was one of these.

The shopping center had been there for at least twenty years, and needed an overhaul and update. It was in the shape of an L with the furniture store on the short leg at the end. It was two stories.

Hawke saw that the furniture store was just closing. He parked in the lot and watched people go into the supermarket, the biggest draw, in the center. A gun store next door to the furniture place had three customers. Two pickups with rifles on racks behind the driver's seat were parked in front of the gun store.

He eased out of the parking space and drove around behind the stores. There was room for trucks and deliveries. He circled the center and parked in the lot well back from the target and two spots over from an exit onto a side street.

Recon and first-hit time. There were two windows showing on the second-floor level of the cutting room at the rear. Both were lighted. The wooden stairway looked well worn. He spotted fifteen cars parked in the area behind the store. Many more than would account for clerks and management.

One straggler came out of the furniture store rear door and keyed two locks. Then he slid into a new Pontiac and drove out the exit. That had to be the manager or owner. Clear below.

He needed a long-range attack point, a firing position. Most of the parking lot was deserted. He could park behind the small cluster of cars that were parked in the lot and have less than a hundred-yard shot. He could nail a fly at that range with the grenade launcher. He drove the van there, parked it so he could fire the M-203 out of the passenger's side window, and locked up the van.

No sense wasting any more time. If the sheep were inside, he had to herd them out before the fun began. How many innocent sheep and how many dirty goats were there inside? He'd have to decide.

Play it by ear.

It was fully dark as he walked up the wooden steps to the

rear door. He tried the door handle silently. Locked. The lock wasn't a difficult type. He took out a set of pics and worked on it for a minute, and it clicked open.

But when he turned the knob and pulled, the door moved only a fraction of an inch. It was bolted from the inside.

He doubled up his fist and pounded on the panel. There was no response. He found a piece of two-by-four lying on the stairs and banged it against the door. Again nothing happened. The second time he gave the door twenty hard whacks with the stick. It was a solid door.

This time a light snapped on over the stairs and a small speaker at the side of the door rasped into life.

"Don't break down the damn door! What the hell you want? Push the button to talk."

Hawke pressed the small red button. "Damn, hard to do a guy a favor these days. There's a fire in the place downstairs. Some guy told me to rush up here and tell you. Doesn't look like the whole place will go up, but he said to be on the safe. . . ."

The door swung open.

A bald man in his forties with thick glasses glared at Hawke.

"No shit? A fire? Downstairs? Christ, what am I going to do?"

"Might be a good idea to get any people up here out until they give you the all clear, I'd say."

"Yeah. I hate to. Behind schedule." The man started to turn.

"I'll take care of your schedule," Hawke said. He pushed the .45 autoloader into the man's side and shoved him into the building.

"What the hell?"

"You just went out of business," Hawke said. The man saw the .45 and spun, trying to slap at it.

The big, unsilenced .45 sounded like a 105 howitzer in the closed room. The heavy slug took the bald man in the side just under his ribs, slanted down through his gut and exited over one hip.

The force of the round jolted him three feet away from Hawke and dumped him on the floor.

There was a partition just beyond the crumpled form. A man pushed his head past the door, saw Hawke holding the gun and the man bleeding on the floor.

"Madre de Dios!" he whispered. He turned and shouted something in Spanish into the room and before Hawke could do more than move out of the way, fifteen people came running out of the room. They looked at the body on the floor and hurried past and down the steps. Some of them crossed themselves as they went past the wounded man.

When they had all left, Hawke looked into the large section of the building. There was one partition, but the rest of the space was taken up by a standard cutting room.

The man on the floor groaned. Hawke knelt beside him and checked the wound. There was a lot of blood. Too much. Gut shot like that he was lucky he had lasted this long.

"Don't ever try to beat a trigger finger again," Hawke told the bald-headed man.

"I won't. Christ, that hurts!"

"You gambled and lost. You don't get a second chance."

"I know." The man coughed. Blood sprayed out of his mouth. He tried to say something, but more blood got in the way. He lay on his side. He eased over on his back and looked up at Hawke.

"You that Avenger?" he asked at last.

"Some people call me that."

"Least no small-time punk . . ."

The man coughed again, blood surged from his mouth,

staining red his chest and the floor around him. The last cough lifted his shoulders six inches off the floor. When he fell back he was dead.

Hawke stared at the body for a moment. He had gambled and lost. Some day that would be him lying there.

But not yet!

He jumped up, ran into the big room, and planted a quarter-pound of C-4 plastic explosive under the machine where the coke and filler were mixed together. He set the pencil timer/detonator for two minutes, pushed the activator, and ran out of the room.

One man at the bottom of the steps looked upward. Hawke hurried down the stairs three at a time.

"The guy up there, he hurt bad?" the white kid who looked about twenty years old asked.

"He's as hurt as he can get. Let's move, this place is going to blow in a minute."

They both ran. Hawke lost the young man in the jumble of cars, then walked on to his van.

Just after he got inside, the roof of the second floor over the hardware store lifted two feet in the air, then a section of it blasted a hundred feet upward as a tremendous explosion shattered the whole building. The sides fell in on the top floor, then the ceiling over the furniture store sagged and fell in. A fire started in one corner and spread quickly.

Hawke angled the M-16 with the M-203 grenade launcher on it and estimated the distance. Then he fired out the window. The first round barely made it over the front wall of the second floor and exploded inside the cutting room with a cracking blast like a hand grenade going off.

People began running around the store. When the grenade went off inside, they shrank back, giving the store a fifty-foot margin of safety.

Far off, a siren screamed as it came closer. Cop or fire engine?

Hawke put a second round into what had once been the top floor of the building. The crowd shrank back farther as the explosion blasted into the residential quietness.

A cop got there first. He pushed the people back farther, talked to some of them, then waved the fire truck in. The men were laying hose when Hawke rammed another round into the burning mass of the building. The firemen stood waiting now, their hoses filled hard with water.

The firemen pointed to the building and shook their heads. Hawke grinned. The grenades had done their work. The firemen would give the fire another five minutes. If no more explosions went off, then they would try to put it out, or to save the building on the far side. Two hoses now were showering water on the gun store next door.

Hawke put the M-16 away in a bench storage seat and drove out the side entrance, in the opposite direction from the fire. In the morning the police would find the remains of the cutting operation and the body. There would be an investigation but the police were so caught up in bureaucracy and legal restrictions that they couldn't be really hard on the druggers. Lopez might even be paying off the police, Hawke thought.

But that was another job. His was getting the drugs *before* anyone could be bribed. If he did that job, the bribery money would dry up—with the rest of the hard cash.

Hawke drove halfway back to his regular parking spot. Habit. A routine—doing the same thing every time, every night—could get a cop, or a DEA agent, killed. He'd stay at a different spot tonight. He picked a light industrial park on his way back downtown and pulled in between two laundry delivery rigs.

Everything was quiet in the lot, no lights showed. He

turned off his engine and turned out his lights. He still had not worked out his whole scenario for battering down Lopez. Every little bit helped. He'd get more nervous, more irritated, and then he might make that one big mistake.

But Hawke wouldn't count on that. He would play out his attack plans, realign them when needed, and work up to his final attack on the big man himself, in his heavily fortified Presidio.

Hawke settled down at the small table with a low light on and worked over his attack plan. He needed to plot strategy and assemble a supply of weapons. Slowly he began to write down ideas of how to hurt Lopez. Soon he began to smile.

CHAPTER TWELVE

Carmelita hummed a tune she had just heard on the radio as she parked her Z at the curb and locked it. She had hated to leave Hawke, but she owed it to herself, and to Diego, to be home tonight. He was going through a tough phase. She remembered one something like it she had struggled with when she had just gotten out of high school.

She took her purse and hurried up the steps to her apartment. It was on a quiet street, a simple little triplex where everyone knew everyone, yet let one another alone.

She grinned when she realized she was humming. She hadn't done that for . . . what? Three or four years. She remembered the wonderfully fulfilling night with Matthew Hawke and her smile widened. What a fine man! Why couldn't something great like this have happened to her before?

She turned her key in the lock and pushed open the door. For a moment a chill ran down her spine. She had always been a little leery of coming into a darkened house or even an unlighted room. All because she had been badly frightened when she was a teenager by a boy inside a dark room. He hadn't meant to scare her, but she screamed and fainted, and to this day she remembered vividly how terrified she had been.

Now Carmelita shrugged, reached around the door jamb, and turned on the lights. See! Nothing unusual or out of the ordinary. Diego wasn't home yet. He must be hot on the trail of a new job.

She closed the door, locked it, and dropped her purse on the chair by the door. That was so she would know exactly where it was when she had to leave quickly in the morning.

Carmelita undressed outside her bedroom. She wanted that long bath with bubbles and lots of warm water and the radio playing softly so she could dream.

She had almost reached her bedroom door when it swung open and a black man, naked to the waist, sprang out of the room and grinned at her. He was the ugliest man she had ever seen and he held a knife that looked a foot long.

Carmelita screamed and screamed. She couldn't stop. Another man came up behind her, put one arm around her chest and grabbed one breast. His other hand clamped down over her mouth, shutting off her screams.

A few seconds later her eyes went wide in terror and she fainted. She came to almost at once. The hand still held her mouth. The man's fingers dug into her right breast. She struggled against him but he was too strong.

"Well now, look at this little poon, would you," the black man said, stroking her breast. "A little spitfire Mex. I like good Mex poon almost as much as black."

He bent and ran his hand up the inside of Carmelita's leg until she kicked at him. He laughed.

"Yeah, a spitfire! I love it. I'm ready right now. Get her

into the bedroom. The man said we could have all the fun we wanted to with this one. Come on, move her!"

The man behind her took his hand off her mouth and let one arm slip out. She clawed out at the black man ahead of her. Her fingernail caught in his cheek and ripped down, dragging flesh and skin with it.

The black screamed and punched her in the jaw.

Carmelita had never felt such a blow. It rocked her back in the man's arms, her knees went on vacation, and her head seemed to be knocked off her shoulders. Strange lights popped on and off and she was so dizzy she couldn't stand.

"Christ, don't knock her head off," the man holding her said. He lifted her in his arms and carried her into the bedroom.

This time it took her a few minutes to regain consciousness. She heard them talking first, then slowly her mind cleared and she opened her eyes.

The black man was naked now, his penis fully erect. Her blouse was unbuttoned and her bra loose. She shivered.

"Hey, our poon done come back to life for us. Damn, she's a looker. Them tits!" He sat down on the bed beside where she lay. She pushed away from him. The other man sat on the other side of her single bed, leaving little room for her to move. He was a Mexican about her age.

"Why are you doing this to me?" she asked in Spanish. The Mexican man shook his head and turned away.

The black slapped her face gently. "None of that Mex talk. You want to talk you speak English, savvy?" The black hands reached for her blouse.

"Now we get on with it, pretty little mama. No good undressing a poon when she's sleeping. Yeah! You got to be awake to enjoy it!"

He watched her push his hands away from her blouse. "Hell, Mondo, you better hold the little cunt's hands. She don't look none too much like she's gonna cooperate. You better, high and mighty. You scratch me again I'll cut both your tits off, you understand that?''

Carmelita shivered then nodded.

''Good. Mondo get her hands, I'm wanting this one real bad.'' He jerked her blouse open and pushed her loose bra up to her throat and grinned at her bare breasts. ''Sit up, poon, I want to see them jutting out there like two sideways mountains!''

Before she had been too terrified to cry. Now she decided that might be the only defense she had left. She cried softly, then wailed.

For a moment she watched his hands tearing at her clothes. They sat her up and ripped her blouse off, then took her bra away and stared.

She wouldn't watch. She looked away. His hands on her were like red-hot iron. She shrank back and he laughed, but she didn't hear him.

Slowly she pulled away, she retreated into a soft, pleasant place where no one could touch her. She faded out of the reality of her bedroom.

Now and then she was aware that she was moved. She knew she was naked at last and that the man hovered over her. But then she faded away again, heard the man swearing, but it wasn't as bad as it had been. She lapsed in and out of consciousness.

After what seemed like hours, she realized that both men had used her two or three times each. It was an uneasy feeling she had now. They talked at the side of the room. Slowly she let herself come back to the present, ordered her mind to take over again. She lay as she had been, watching them from slitted eyes. They both were dressing, laughing.

What they said made no sense. Something about how the big payoff was still to come. The fun was over, now they had to earn their money. Money? What were they talking about.

"Here?" Mondo asked.

"Hell no, not here. You a damn amateur at this work. Never here. Makes too many problems."

The black man looked in her closet, found a robe and threw it at her.

"Put this on, now!"

She sat up.

"Yeah, them are nice tits!" he said. He shook his head. "A damn shame, but can't be helped. Bought and paid for."

"What?"

"Nothing, poon. Don't worry about it. Get your robe on, we're going for a drive."

"I'm not moving!" Carmelita shouted.

He hit her. The slap slammed her sideways on the bed and she rolled over. Mondo stood on the other side of the bed.

"Put on the robe, it'll be easier," he said softly.

She looked up at him in disbelief. "You raped me, now you're being kind? What kind of an animal are you?"

"Just doing what I have to do," the young Mexican said.

Carmelita put on the robe.

They drove through the Houston night and soon Carmelita wasn't sure where they were.

Ten minutes later they eased through a truck door into a warehouse and stopped. Lights came on and Mondo pulled her out of the car. She could hear men around but couldn't see anyone. Mondo sat her down in a chair in a small room and three men came in. She didn't know any of them.

All three were Mexicans.

"You know Matt Hawke?" a tall slender man asked her.

"I want my clothes, and I want out of here right now. Are you the man in charge?"

Someone from the side slapped her. She swayed to the right and Mondo caught her. He stood her up and stripped the robe from her. She stood there naked, embarrassed, angry, and now so frightened she wasn't sure if she could speak.

The man asked her the question again in the same tone of voice, as if nothing had happened.

She took her hand down from her face where she had touched her sore cheek. She had to answer or they would figure out some way to hurt her.

"Yes," she said softly.

The tall man smiled. "Good, Carmelita, good. Now we are making progress. This man has been very bad to me lately, and I need to know where he is staying. You know and I want you to tell me. He recently changed vans. What's the license number on the new one and what does it look like?"

"I don't know the license number. I don't remember what kind of a van it was."

Someone held her firmly from behind. A knife came into her vision. Some liquid on the blade burned brightly. The knife lowered and made a three-inch slice across her right breast. The fluid burning on the knife ran off into the slice and burned fiercely.

Carmelita screamed. A brown hand clamped over her mouth and nose, then gradually allowed her to breathe through her nose.

The knife slash had sent a terrible shock wave through her system, a deadly gush of pain that smothered her rational thought and made her cry out.

The instant that the flaming fluid fell into the quarter-inch-deep cut her brain seemed to explode with signals of agonizing pain from her breast. Thousands of nerve endings flared and reported the sensation of burning.

Somehow she did not faint. She looked down past the wrist holding her under her chin. She could see her right breast and the line of fire there. A gradual mental detachment started to come again, then she beat it back. *No!* She was going to stay here and fight them!

Slowly the flame burned out. There was no blood. The flame had cauterized the open wound as it burned itself up. It reminded her of seeing flame throwers burning lighter fluid on their hands. They said it didn't hurt. They lied. They simply endured the pain.

"Now, Carmelita. You see how serious we are. We want to know exactly where Hawke has parked his van, and what he plans to do next. I am not a patient man, miss. You must understand that."

Stall them. Talk. Tell them everything, yet nothing. Confuse them. Yes!

"All right. Don't burn me again. Please don't. I left Hawke at Broad Fern just off Freeway 45, the Gulf Freeway. But he moves around. He calls when we meet. I don't know where he is now. He might be out working. He never tells me. And that's the truth! I can't tell you what I don't know!"

There was some hushed talk in the background, out of the lights.

Carmelita had been a model for a short time. She was somewhat used to lights and people looking at her, but she had never done any lingerie work or nude shots. Now that some of the shock had worn off she was embarrassed and furious. The open slash on her breast was starting to sting and burn and throb as the shock wore off and the still-whole nerves responded to the continuing trauma.

"Where do you usully meet him, Carmelita?"

"At Broad Fern and Freeway 45."

"You're lying, Carmelita!"

Someone reached in and grabbed her burned breast and twisted it until she screamed. The hand let go and she sobbed. She couldn't stop.

"Where was Hawke going tonight?"

"I don't know. He didn't tell me."

"You're lying!"

Hands forced her legs apart and someone grabbed her crotch from below and squeezed. Her scream so surprised the man that he let go of her tender area.

Carmelita fought against fainting. She was afraid if she passed out now that she would never be alive again. She had to fight them!

The hands holding her let go and she weaved for a moment to get her balance.

The tall man with the sharp features nodded.

"Carmelita, you may be telling the truth after all. You go have a rest and we'll talk later."

When they led her away, the tall man in charge looked pensive.

"We may have enough about him now. We'll need her later for the phone call, so be sure she's in good shape."

"When will he call?"

"As soon as he finds out we have her. Probably not until the morning sometime. You left a note in her apartment with the telephone number to call?"

"Yes sir, Mr. Lopez. Two notes, big ones. Nobody can miss them."

"All right. Get out of here. Remember she has to be able to talk and sound normal tomorrow morning."

"Right, Mr. Lopez," the man said and hurried after the others. They had all night to play sexy games with this beautiful lady! He rubbed his crotch in anticipation.

Ahead of him down a hallway, one of the men opened the door and turned on a light. He gave Carmelita her robe and she walked into the ten-foot-square room. There was a bed, a dresser and a TV set. To one side she saw a small bath.

"Lopez said for you to rest," he said. He closed the door and she heard it lock. She looked quickly but saw that there was no lock on the inside and nothing she could use to block the door.

Slowly she walked across the room and sat on the bed. With a burst of tears she fell on the bed, caught a pillow, and cried into it. How in the world had this happened? Why were they torturing her?

Because of Matthew Hawke.

For a moment she thought of Hawke's wife in San Diego and the suffering she must have endured. At once she shut that out of her mind. She told herself she would be all right. She had told them all they wanted to know, everything she knew.

Slowly she began to relax. Gradually she let the waves of mental and emotional exhaustion wash over her and she snuggled against the pillow. Soon she was sleeping.

Outside in the hallway the men made bets, flipped a coin for a winner, and then watched through a crack of the open door. When she had been sleeping for a half-hour, they moved into the room.

The bets had been made, the money covered. Juan had won at the coin toss. It was up to him to try to make love to the pretty woman before she came fully awake.

It began for Carmelita as a bad dream. She pushed at the hands, brushed away the caresses, lifted hands away from her breasts. But slowly her desire began to grow. She thought it was Hawke then and she cooperated for a moment, a giggle penetrating her sleepy mind.

Then she came awake in a rush, and screamed at the man poised between her spread legs.

"Noooooooooooooooooooooo!" she bellowed, and flung the slender man off the bed to the floor.

The men laughed and howled. Some swore and paid off the bets. Juan stood up and glared at her. He grabbed her ankles and spread them wide on the bed and pointed at men to hold them. Two more men held her wrists high over her head.

"Now we see who laughs at Juan!" he said. "Six times easy with this *puta*. Then you all get a turn."

The men laughed and whooped as Juan knelt on the bed.

This time Carmelita spit in Juan's face and then took his vicious slap. The sting of that slap was the last thing she felt as she lost consciousness.

CHAPTER THIRTEEN

It was nearly midnight when Hawke stepped out of his rented van and looked down the street. In the industrial area there were few phones. He spotted one next to a small closed cafe.

He should call Carmelita, let her know that he wouldn't be at the usual meeting spot. He didn't want her to worry in the morning. The phone rang four times before anyone picked it up. Then the voice came softly, with anger and fear showing through. It was Diego.

"Yes?"

"Diego. This is Hawke. Is Carmelita there?"

"Oh God! I hoped that she was with you." There was something that sounded like strangled sobbing. "He got her, then. The damn note must be true!"

"Diego, what are you talking about?"

"I got home about eleven. Lights out, door unlocked, place messed up. Carm not here. Then I find a note scrawled in pencil. It says "Matthew Hawke. We've got

Carmelita. You want her safe, you call this number for directions what to do."

Sweat popped out on Hawke's forehead. *Dammit! Not again!*

"Now, Diego. Take it easy. Does it look like a fight, a struggle in the house?"

"Yeah, and cigarette butts all over. We don't smoke. Some guys waited here for a long time."

"All right. Diego. Did you read the note to me exactly the way it was written?"

"Yeah. Exactly."

"What was that phone number?"

"Why should I tell you! You got her into this trouble!"

"Easy, Diego. Are you going to try to rescue her? They wrote the note to me. They expect me to call. Now give me the phone number."

Diego read it off and Hawke wrote it down on the back of a small pad.

"Diego. I'm not sure where I'll be, but you get out of there. I'll call and find out what they want. Probably money. I've got some. You be sure to stay with one of your friends tonight. I'll contact you there tomorrow. Just stay cool. Carmelita will be fine."

"Fine? How the hell you know? Kidnapping, hostage. That's pretty rough stuff. If anything happens to her, it's all your fault, man! Nothing like this happened before you came. I'm warning you, man! Carmelita is hurt, I'm getting a gun and I'm coming after you!"

"I understand how you feel, Diego. I'm just as sorry as you are, but this is going to work out. I have the number, I'll call them. Now get out of there."

They hung up. Hawke looked at the phone but was unable to control his anger. He slammed the receiver back into the holder and broke it. Hawke didn't notice the smashed phone as he stormed out of the phone booth, his mind reeling.

Now they had two hostages!

They knew they could get to him by taking Carmelita. He ran down the block to burn off some of his fury. He couldn't call them right now. He had to calm down. He ran three blocks and, panting, he eased to a stop. A car came down the street and he faded into some shadows of the industrial section.

It was a Houston Police car, but it kept on going on its patrol without the cops inside seeing him.

Lopez must be the one who had her. He couldn't know who was hitting his places, but he probably figured that Hawke was in on some of it. Hawke would demand to hear Carmelita's voice. He had to know that she was safe. If they hurt her . . .

He walked another block, found a phone, and dialed the number.

"Yeah?"

"I'm calling about Carmelita Salazar. You kidnapped her tonight."

"You catch on fast. Just a minute."

The line went silent. Thirty seconds later a new voice came on, smoother, more refined, educated.

"This must be Mr. Matthew Hawke himself I'm talking to," the voice said.

"Who the hell are you?" Hawke spat.

"You're in no position to ask questions, Hawke. Just shut up and listen to your instructions."

"Hell, no. First I want to know that Carmelita is safe and unharmed. Put her on the phone right now, or I'm walking."

"Hold it! Wait a minute. Yes. We can put her on the phone. It may take a minute or two. She's probably sleeping by now. Hold on right there, I'll get her on the extension in about two minutes."

"Go."

Hawke stared at the plastic phone. He had told himself that never again would he let a friend get in trouble because of him, especially not a woman. Now it had happened.

It was Lopez' move. Damn all the druggers! Hawke thought, everyone selling drugs should be shot within twenty-four hours of capture. Forget the niceties of the law. Wipe out a few thousand of these gutter rats, and the rest of them would think twice about selling the poison.

Hawke couldn't understand how rational human beings could put that poison in their systems. It was worse than taking a knife and cutting yourself. They wouldn't do that, but they kept right on cutting up their insides, becoming dependent on drugs, and going steadily downhill. Why didn't these people stop and think what they were doing to their bodies!

"Okay, Hawke, she's here. She was sleeping, but we have her awake and at the phone. Don't try to ask her a lot of questions because we won't let her answer. She's going to say hello, let you respond, then give you her name and address and a couple more sentences, then you'll know that she's alive and well. You try anything else and I'll cut her off. I'm on the extension. Here she is."

Hawke cleared his throat.

"Carm? Carmelita?"

"Yes, Hawke, I'm here." Her voice was soft, disinterest-ed, as if she had given up.

"Are you all right? Have they hurt you?"

"I'm alive, Hawke, and I want you to come get me. That's all they said I can say. Goodbye, Hawke."

That was all.

"Now, Hawke, you heard her, you know she's safe and

well and we're taking care of her. Your job is to come and pick her up. We know you have that two million dollars from that briefcase you took off our men. You bring that, and we'll trade you the cash for the girl."

Hawke didn't say a word. The line was silent a moment.

"Hey, we're not animals. We're businessmen. We have something you want. You have something we want, so we trade one for the other. Are you still there, Hawke?"

"Yes, keep talking."

"I'm going to give you directions, and a time to meet, and we want you to come alone, unarmed and ready to cooperate in the trade. Anything else will mean big trouble for both you and the girl. Do you understand?"

"Yeah, you're holding the aces, what else can I do?"

"Now you're making sense, Hawke. Here's exactly what I want you to do."

Hawke listened to the demands again, and the time and place of the meeting. He memorized the details. They would probably always be burned into his memory. But even as the specifics were being spelled out, he was setting up a plan.

It was about one A.M. when he walked back to his camper. He got in and kicked the engine into life.

They had given him too much lead time. The meeting was set for daylight, five hours away. He had plenty of time to survey the meeting spot, pick out any problem areas, locate the best spots to hide, and to work out a plan of attack.

But when he got to the address he found it to be the Worthham Golf Course, just off the Gulf Freeway and not far from the University of Houston. He was to come at the golf course from Polk Road, cross South Wayside Street and get into the fairway. There was a small stream called Club Bayou just south of there.

The meet would take place on the tee nearest to the end of the bayou, the contact man didn't know the number.

Hawke was told to be there exactly at dawn, because a half-hour later the place would be swarming with foursomes charging around the course in the cool of the early morning.

Hawke would be there all right. He parked well away from the place he planned to enter the course. For a moment he puzzled over what weapons he should take. At last he decided he had to take the M-16 and grenade launcher, a quarter pound of C-4 and detonators, and his trusty .45 auto-loader. He put eight HE rounds of the 40-mm grenades in his ammo bag and slipped it over his shoulder.

For this mission he changed into black: a black, long-sleeved jersey pullover, black pants, and his half-boots. He put his .45 on a web belt cinched around his waist and added a special ammo pouch that held two of the fourteen-round .45 magazines.

On his head he put a black baseball cap. He used a cammo stick to blacken his face until it showed only streaks and glints of white. On his hands he pulled a pair of thin black leather gloves that were as tight as a second skin.

Outside his van, Hawke stopped and watched the street. It was about two A.M. Nothing moved. A car went along the main stem next to the golf course now and then.

He jogged to South Wayside, waited a moment for a car to clear, then rushed across the wide avenue and up to the golf course. At one point, near where a small stream went under the fence, the barrier was low enough for Hawke to climb up and leap over.

Lopez' men would not bring Carmelita in by that route. They probably wanted to pin him against the fence if he tried to resist them.

At first he had thought it might be an even trade. He could save Carmelita's life if he came to the meet. But nothing of the kind was mentioned. He refused to believe that they would hurt the girl. She had nothing to do with this fight.

They must know that.

Exactly!

They knew that and had used it to their advantage, knowing that he would show up. They would use every plus they could against him. Slowly he realized that a lot of time would have passed between his talk with Carmelita and the money-trade time. A lot of bad things could happen to the lady.

He had never considered trading the money for Carmelita. He would have them both, to hurt Alejandro even more. He had brought along the same attaché case he had rescued from the country place on the ship's channel. But he had left the money in the van. It would work. They would go for the case.

Hawke let his combat senses take over. He stashed the empty case by the fence in some tall weeds, slung the M-16 over his shoulder, and ran south toward the bend in the small stream. It ended about fifty yards into the golf course and worked its way through three water hazards.

He spotted the first tee, and the one nearest the twisting, winding stream. It was just as they had described it. The meet would be there. There was a small rise toward the street. Hawke ran that way, found what he wanted, and nodded. He ran back for the attaché case and hid it behind a tree, then he planned his attack.

The more he checked the lay of the land, the sweeping bunkers and fairways and rows of trees outlining things, the more sure he was that Alejandro was setting him up for a kill. They would come about four A.M. with long guns and zero in on the tee, expecting him to waltz into their gunsights.

The high ground where he stood was a prime sniper location to hit the tee. Where were two others?

He found them after a quick tour. There was a restroom on the edge of the next green over. From the side of it a marksman would have a clear shot at the tee. He stopped beside the block building and cut in half the quarter pound of C-4 plastic explosive.

Carefully he formed the soft explosive around one of the HE 40-mm grenades. He put a number-one electronic detonator into the soft coating of the small but deadly bomb and lay it against the foundation of the small building. Hawke covered it with grass and some withered leaves until it was not noticeable.

From his pocket he took out a small black box the size of a pack of cards and keyed the number-one switch to "on." Now one more movement of the switch to "fire," and the powerful little radio sending device would transmit a radio signal to the small antenna on the detonator he had pushed into the explosive and it would explode.

The radio detonator had four channels.

The next spot he found with good protection and good firing-sight lines to the tee was a trio of evergreen trees in a small triangle where one fairway did a dog leg away from him. The best spot would be beside the largest tree. A gunner could stand or lie there and have a great shot at the tee.

Hawke planted a second radio controlled bomb there. It was made like the first one, and he keyed in the number-two switch on the black box.

As to the high ground he had claimed, he figured it would be the first spot selected. Which meant he had to be invisible for a while.

The slight rise was not more than twenty yards from the fence here. He walked it for thirty yards until he found what he wanted, a spot where runoff water had gouged out a small rut in the rough, which the tractor-ridden mowers had trouble getting across. So around the ditch had grown a border of two-foot-high grass and weeds.

Hawke settled into the two-foot-deep gully and peered through the growth at the number-one ambush point he had just left. He had a perfect view. He settled down in his new home. He would have a wait, but he was used to waiting.

Once in 'Nam he had lain in a swamp for four hours waiting for a patrol of North Vietnamese to finish a rest break and move on down the road.

As he waited now he kept wide awake. This was no time to sleep himself to death. If Lopez' man had any sense at all he would come early and scout the area, at least place his snipers in position.

Hawke had no way of knowing if the voice on the phone belonged to a man with any 'Nam experience, or even any military training. In a way he hoped that the man was a good combat man. That would give Hawke all the more pleasure in blowing him away.

He touched the black box in his ammo pouch. He had taken the magazines out of it and dropped them in his ammo bag. The little black box could make a big difference in this affair.

Hawke tried not to think about Connie as he waited. She was gone, tortured to death in the most terrible, pain-filled death anyone could imagine.

And the bastards were going to pay for it! Pay again and again!

Just as he began to think about Carmelita, to worry about her, he saw a car stop along the golf course fence. Three men got out, lifted some equipment over the fence and climbed over it. Then the car raced away.

Hawke watched as best he could in the dim light. The

moon had not favored him with more than half a slice tonight. At least there were no clouds.

The three men made a lot of noise as they came across the fence. One of them yelled as he fell and the others laughed. Hawke could see them all crouching just inside the fence. They each carried something which could be a rifle.

They walked to the tee the same way Hawke had done. In the faint moonlight he saw them pointing out hiding spots. The taller of the trio spoke sharply as if he had the last say. He took one man into the triangle of trees, and Hawke grinned.

The second man was spotted not beside the restroom, but behind a low block wall that hid two garbage cans and a ball washer.

The larger man talked to the second man for half an hour, then he moved up to the high ground where Hawke had guessed he would. Two out of three wasn't bad.

The man simply stretched out on the grass. He was slightly down the reverse slope of the rise, so a man standing on the tee could not see him.

Hawke grinned. Positioning himself that way put the drugger less than twenty-five yards away. Not a bad shot for the silenced .45. With fourteen rounds he should be able to put him out of action and take his place.

The ex-DEA agent watched the head man closely. He could see no use of a radio. There was no other means of communicating with his two hit men. They had been given their instructions and now would wait for the attack signal.

In the same situation, Hawke would tell his men to fire only after he fired the first shot.

It was just a little after four forty-five. It would be dawn in another half-hour.

Hawke pulled out the .45 from the holster, took the

silencer from his ammo bag and screwed it into place. He tested a wetted finger for wind.

Absolutely none. Rise, fall? The man was about ten feet above him, a rising shot.

Before Hawke could sight in on the bushwhacker with his silenced .45, he heard a motor of some kind. The sound came from deeper into the golf course.

Then he recognized it. It was one of the electric golf carts charging across the grass toward the spot where the men lay hidden.

The golf cart went directly to the tee. The driver bailed out, left the rig there and ran back to the edge of the restroom, and stood directly over Hawke's number two bomb.

Carmelita must be on the golf cart, probably tied up. He sighted in on the man on the reverse slope, allowing a little for the uphill shot. He squeezed off the round, then pulled the .45 back on target and fired again.

He fired six times, and the shooter on the hill let out a low yell and twisted to stand up. The last shot brought him down and dumped him to the side where he writhed a moment, then lay still.

"What the hell?" one of the guards called.

"Ronko. You okay?" the closer man called.

Hawke took out the little black box and crawled out of the weeds toward the high ground he wanted. The shooter had not moved since he rolled over. Hawke made it to a spot where he could see the three spots where his enemies were hidden.

As quickly as he could, he moved the switch on the first and second transmission positions, and in a millisecond, two explosions rocked the quiet dampness of the Houston night. It was just starting to get light.

Hawke saw the man near the tree thrown through the air.

He turned to watch the spot by the restroom. Half of the blocks on the wall beside the bomb shattered. The man who had been standing there cartwheeled a dozen feet away, one arm missing entirely as he slammed into the soft green grass of the fairway.

Hawke concentrated on watching the spot where the other shooter had hidden, behind the garbage can holder.

"Christ! What the hell is going on? We in a war?" the man shouted. There was no one to answer him.

"Pepé, Juan!" What the hell happened?" He stood up a minute to stare at the rise where the other man should have been.

"Juan, I'm getting out of here!" he called.

Hawke's trigger finger squeezed and three rounds from the M-16 slammed into the drugger's chest, snuffing out his life in a fraction of a second and jolting him six feet from where he had stood.

Hawke knew the enemy were all down. He came up running, charging ahead for the tee where he had been supposed to die. Now all he had to do was get Carmelita and charge away from here before the golf course people or the Houston cops showed up to find out what the explosions and the gunshots were all about.

At the tee he hesitated. The golf cart sat sideways, the way the driver had left it. Slumped in the front seat sat a woman. Hawke rushed up. She was not tied in.

He turned her face and saw she was Carmelita. His hand jerked back.

NO!

Her face had been cold to his touch! He fought back tears as he reached in and rested his fingers on her throat. There was no pulse! She was dead. Her face was unmarked.

Now he realized that she wore only a bathrobe. He

opened the front of it and saw the burns, the knife slices, and the two small purple holes over her heart!

"Noooooooooooooooooooooooooooooooo, not again!" Hawke bellowed into the brightening sky. He heard a siren from a long way off.

He bent and touched the pale cheek. Tears spilled from his eyes. "I'm sorry, Carmelita. I promised myself this wouldn't happen to you. I'm sorry. Now they're going to pay double! All of these bastards are going to pay twice!" Automatically he checked his equipment, then ran for the fence.

Now he had to get away. If he wanted to pay them back he had to clear the area fast. He found the same place he came in, climbed the fence and knelt on the far side.

As he turned to look back at the scene, he could see a golf cart and the bouncing shape of a pickup with lights on charging toward the scene. He lifted up and walked across South Wayside. There was still little traffic. No one would remember him.

He walked down two blocks to his van, stashed the weapons, and drove away to the west on Polk Street. Anywhere to put some distance between him and the death scene.

Diego!

He had to find the kid before somebody else told him. Diego would blame Hawke for his sister's murder, he was sure. He had to get it straight. Hawke stormed down Polk Street looking for a telephone he could use.

"Please be home, kid," Hawke said to himself again and again, as he parked and ran for a phone booth.

CHAPTER FOURTEEN

Hawke let the phone ring twenty times to make sure. Diego had gone to stay at a friend's house as he suggested. That made it impossible for Hawke to find the young man. But he had to get in touch with him quickly.

The only thing he could do was go to the apartment and wait for Diego to come. This had to come first!

He drove there at once, parked near the apartment, and began his watch. His only hope was that Diego would come back early in the morning. As he waited he cleaned the black off his face.

Hawke was worried about how Diego would react. Somehow Hawke had to convince the young man that Lopez' men had been responsible for the murder.

Hawke dozed, then decided to go to sleep until six-thirty. He had the ability to wake up at a given time. It was a talent he had worked at over the years.

When he came awake on the van's bed, he saw that it was

light already. He turned on the radio and caught an all-news station.

"... and the Astros swept the home stand three games to zero. In other local news, police still have no clues about what happened on the Worthham Golf Course sometime last night. Two explosions were reported and shots were fired.

"By the time police arrived there were five dead bodies on and around the twelfth tee. Investigators say one of the victims, a woman, had been dead for three or four hours before police arrived. The other four had died only minutes before.

"Late word on the case indicates three and maybe four different weapons were used in the deaths, including a .45 caliber pistol, a smaller hand gun, a rifle of some sort, explosives and perhaps hand grenades. The investigation is continuing. None of the victims' names has been released."

Hawke snapped off the radio. There was no sign of Diego yet. The kid had to come home soon!

Halfway across town two hours later, three of Lopez' top lieutenants came out of a restaurant known for its lavish breakfasts. The three well-dressed Mexicans stood a moment on the sidewalk in front of the eatery, talking.

A car jolted out of the parking lot, swept in front of the three men, and a submachine gun chattered off twenty rounds. The weapon fired out of the car's open window, less than ten feet from the victims.

All three men went down in the hail of high-powered lead. One lived for almost an hour. The other two died on the spot.

When Lopez heard of the killings, he pondered slowly in his big chair behind his desk in the Presidio.

"Four good men died last night, and now three more today? It has never been this deadly. What is happening to my control?'' He took a pen and drew circles and squares on a pad of paper. He had to think.

It could not all be this *diablo*, this Hawke. He outgunned the men last night at the golf course, but not this morning.

Hermano! It had to be that sneaking rat, Hermano. He used the restaurant as well. He knew these three men often had breakfast there and talked business. It had to be Hermano. Time for another hit at the river rat! A blow at his downtown offices. But how? Hermano had a thick security system.

Lopez sat back in his big chair and considered it. He would deal with one problem at a time; first, Hermano.

The main entrance was down a long alley that ended in the outer fringe of the Hermano secure area. What he needed was a small force of blind sheep who would do what he wanted them to, to draw out the Hermano forces without loss to his own men.

Lopez began to smile for the first time that morning. Yes, it would work, and with almost no danger to his own men. It would be an all-out attack. His men would have Uzi submachine guns for their longer range. Yes!

Alejandro picked up his telephone and made three calls to set the operation in motion. The quicker the better!

Far across town, Hawke gave up on the apartment around nine o'clock. He drove around, came back past the apartment, then made another swing. About ten he stopped near the broken fence by the auto salvager. There was a chance that Diego had drifted back to the Toros. He had nothing else now as an anchor, a home.

Hawke slipped through the fence, paused and checked the area, but saw no one. The old bus door was closed. He ran to it and pushed, and it opened easily. No one was inside. He looked around out of curiosity. What did they do here?

As he hesitated inside, he heard footsteps outside. Someone ran up to the door and jumped in.

"Hey, guys sorry that I'm . . ."

"Late . . ." Hawke filled it in. "Where is everyone?"

"Who the hell are you?"

"I'm a friend of Diego's."

"Yeah, the guy with the fancy footwork. He isn't here."

"Where is he?"

"Can't say."

Hawke moved faster than the seventeen-year-old thought he could. He caught the kid's left arm and spun it behind his back.

"Now, you want a broken arm, or just the shoulder joint popped out of its socket?"

"Easy! Shit! Easy!"

"Where are they? They have some action going down this morning?"

"Yeah."

"Where?"

"They'll kill me if I tell you."

"They'll never know. What's happening?"

"Damn, let go and I'll tell you!" The kid's eyes bulged, his face was red. Hawke eased up on the pressure.

"What's happening?"

"Just a job to mess up three guys. It's somewhere near the downtown section. I got the address. Nothing big. We go down this alley and call out these three guys. Tell them they're on our turf and we beat the shit out of them and leave."

"That's it?"

"Hell, that's enough. We only get two hundred for it, but it's a start."

"Yeah, a start to get to prison. What's the address? When are you supposed to meet there?"

"Ten-thirty. We meet then and go down this street or alley or something. I've got the address. Can I have back my arm now?"

Hawke let go. The kid took out a folded piece of paper and showed it to Hawke.

"I was taking a shower, my mom took the message."

It was the 1500 block on Carson Street. Hawke memorized the address.

"Ten-thirty, right. You better hurry if you want to get there in time for the fun." Hawke turned and ran out of the bus through the fence and into his rented van. He better hurry, too, or Diego might be taking the worst step in his young life.

He found the street on his map, then drove there as fast as the law allowed. He couldn't afford a traffic ticket now. Carson Street was on the edge of the business section, where it turned into apartments and smaller stores and light industrial buildings.

The 1500 address was more like a district. It started on the street and wound back into a *cul de sac*, or more like a blind alley with a few back doors on it.

Hawke had a bad feeling as he parked and edged into the start of the alley. Three doors down he saw a cluster of ten people . . . the Toros.

Before Hawke could get up to them, they walked into the alley, spread themselves across the twenty-foot width, and began marching slowly toward the far end, maybe two hundred feet away. Each of the gang members swung a bike chain or held a knife or club. It was going to be an old-fashioned rumble, and somebody would get hurt!

Hawke edged along the side of the alley, taking advantage of the differences in building length. The boys were a hundred feet ahead of him when they stopped, thirty feet from the end of the passage.

"Hard-ass, get your bucket out here!" one of the boys bellowed. A door opened a crack, then closed. After a moment the kid yelled the challenge again.

A well-dressed man stepped from the doorway. He held a shotgun in his hands and it was pointed at the boys.

"Who is the big mouth?" he asked in a clear, loud voice.

Hawke moved up closer behind the boys. He heard noises above him and behind him, but didn't have time to check.

"We want a cat named Romero," the Toro spokesman shouted.

"He don't work here anymore," the man at the doorway said. "Now get smart and turn around and walk out before you're carried out."

"That a threat?"

"A warning." The man waved his arm and windows opened over him and men appeared there, and in doorways, and streamed out the door behind him, until there were twenty men, all with guns aimed at the boys.

"Christ!" one of the Toros said.

Behind him Hawke heard more sounds. He turned just as he caught the flash of the men at windows. They were behind and over those in the alley.

The firing began almost at once from behind and above Hawke.

"Back this way!" Hawke bellowed.

Four of the men standing facing the boys went down, shot dead. The men in the windows and in front of the building returned fire.

Hawke pulled out his .45 and blasted a clip up at the windows behind him, shattering a number, driving some shooters to cover.

"This way!" Hawke shouted again. Diego saw him and ran toward him not to get away, but in fury. The rest of the gang followed him. Two caught bullets. One limped, another held his shoulder.

Hawke found a door at the side and jerked it open. It was a long hallway.

"In here!" he bellowed. "Somebody set you up in a trap!"

Diego dove at Hawke, who caught him and spun him around and shoved him into the hall. The eight other Toros charged in behind him and soon he was swept forward. Hawke grabbed the last kid, the one with a bullet in his leg, and pulled him inside.

They went through the hallway that had doors opening off it, and to the street. By the time they got out, Hawke was half-carrying the shot-up Toro.

Diego was in his face in a second.

"You killed her!" he screamed, and swung the bike chain that he still held in his hand.

Hawke had seen chains before. He dodged the missile and slammed his fist down on Diego's forearm. Diego screeched in pain and the chain fell to the sidewalk.

"Hey, man!" the leader of the gang shouted. "He just saved your ass! He saved all of us. We were in the middle of a damn war in there. We damn lucky to get out of that alley with both our balls still hanging." The leader's right wrist was in a cast.

Diego held his wrist. It wasn't broken.

"You killed her!" he said again, more in control but still furious. "The cops came to the apartment early. They told me what happened. If she'd never even seen you, she'd be alive today, working in the travel agency."

He stormed at Hawke, swung his fist, but Hawke caught it and grabbed the angry young man.

"I'm sorry, Diego. Carmelita was a special person. She was doing this for her friend, for Mrs. Johnson. She literally gave her life to help a friend. I tried to keep her out of the danger. I guess just knowing me was danger enough for her. Lopez did it. Four of them will never hurt anyone else again."

One of the Toros looked up. "Hey, you mean you snuffed them four Lopez drug guys out on the golf course?"

Hawke ignored him. "Diego. How would Carmelita have wanted you to handle something like this?"

"Hey, man, we better move out of here," the Toro leader said. "Them cats we called out ain't gonna be happy."

Hawke motioned to the left down the street. He caught Diego by the shoulders and urged him along the sidewalk.

"How did you guys get messed up in that war?" Hawke asked.

"This dude came up to us in the park," the leader said. "Asked us if we wanted to make an easy two hundred bucks. Hell, we said sure. He told us the time and place, gave us a hundred up front and split. We was there."

"One side in this drug war used you guys for sucker bait," Hawke said. "The guys who hired you probably figured at least half of you would wind up dead, but they didn't care. They just needed those other men to come out in the open. You guys fingered the bunch."

"Christ! We better stay out of sight for at least a week," the leader growled.

"A month would be safer," Hawke said.

"Without this cat we'd still be back there in that alley getting shot up," another of the Toros said.

They walked two more blocks away from the firefight. Sirens had been wailing behind them. At last they stopped and each of the Toros came up and shook Hawke's hand.

"We don't forget favors, man," one of them said.

"Diego damn lucky to have you for a friend," another one added.

When the last of them walked off along the street, Diego still leaned against the wall. His anger at Hawke seemed burned out. His shoulders slumped. He kept shaking his head.

"She's really gone! Carmelita is dead. I never . . . never thought she would leave me." He turned to Hawke. "When the cops told me I stormed out of the house and ran all the way to the bus. The guys were there. They told me what they had working. I have nobody else. The Toros are my only family now."

"I bet a guy like you can do better than the Toros. What happened to that job?"

"Oh, yeah. I got an interview." He looked at his wristwatch. "Damn. I'm supposed to be there at noon."

"Plenty of time."

"No." He stood a little straighter. "My sister. The last of our family. I have to make the arrangements. We talked about that once. She said no funeral, even if we are Catholic. She said just a cremation and maybe a memorial service." He paused, took the headband off, and threw it on the ground. All of the Toros wore them, a bright red splash of cloth.

"I'll go see the priest. Haven't been to church for a while, but he's a good guy. He'll help me do it."

They walked a little farther.

"You going to be all right?"

Diego looked up at him, black eyes flashing. "Yeah. All right. Got some things to do. Then I'm going to try to find that guy who hired us in the park. I've seen him with some of Lopez' pushers. He's some kind of big shot in the coke distribution system. When I find him . . ."

Hawke held up his hand. "That's my business. I'm a pro at it, Diego. Have you ever killed a man?"

Diego shook his head.

"I have, more than one. I know how hard it is. I know how it twists the gut and makes you think just how puny man is on this planet. Leave the killing to the professionals. Carmelita would have told you that. Right?"

Diego nodded.

"Yeah, she would."

"You talk to the priest. Make your arrangements, and then go back and see about that job, or get another one. I've got some money that I owe Carmelita; I better give it to you." Hawke took out the roll of hundreds from his pocket and gave it to Diego.

"This should be enough to tide you over until you get working."

Diego looked at the hundred on the outside. His eyes went wide. Then he flipped through the roll.

"Jesus! Must be thousands in here!"

"About four thousand. Take care of it. Be sure the priest tells Mrs. Johnson about Carmelita. She may have had some kind of insurance where she worked."

Hawke turned and took a step away.

"Get going. I have another job. Some exterminating to do. I have a double payback now for those bastards!"

Diego looked up, surprised by the anger, the just-controlled rage that showed through Hawke's words.

"Hey, you be careful. I . . . I don't have so many friends I can afford to lose another one." He turned and then came back. "Besides, we've got a fishing date on Saturday."

Diego walked away, both hands in his pockets but with his shoulders squared.

He was going to be fine, Hawke decided. The kid would come through in great shape.

Now for that exterminating job.

CHAPTER FIFTEEN

Hawke drove downtown after he left Diego. He had to park six blocks away from the Paper Man's stand. He walked up and tossed a quarter in the change box and took a *Houston Post*.

"Thank you, suh," the Paper Man said.

"You're welcome."

"I didn't quite understand what you said."

Hawke grinned at the subservient tone in the old black man's voice. "I only said that you were welcome. Do you recognize my voice now or should I talk some more?"

The Paper Man chuckled. "The Suntan Man from the Land of Pacific Sunshine. Hear you've been busy."

"Now and then when I get work."

"You lied to me the other day," the Paper Man said.

"I did? How was that?"

"Done told me that was a single dollar bill you asked me to make change for."

"Oh, that," said Hawke. "Just a whim. I'm a sucker for a down-and-out story."

"Damn! It still works." The Paper Man laughed. "You ever heard of the Maxim Variable Annuity from Great West? Case you haven't, it's an investment plan. Has a bond fund, a growth fund in hot stocks, and a government-guaranteed fund. Just to set your heart at ease, I've got enough in all three to buy out half that city block behind you. Ain't general knowledge."

Hawke grinned. "Won't tell a soul."

"Good. Gave that hundred in cash to my three young friends who do clean-up work for me. I used to have trouble with young punks hassling me. Now I hire these three boys to watch out for me down here. Never a problem."

"Glad to hear it. Now I've got a problem. I'm fresh out of targets. You hear anything on the streets about a crash house for mules?"

"The big boys have them all over town. Move the guys around so much. Did hear about one you might like. Used to be a small apartment house. About ten, twelve apartments. Lopez sets it up. He's got a woman who rents furniture or buys it, furnishes the place, hires a cook and caretaker. The mules come in and crash there until they have another job moving goods across the border down at Brownsville or heading up the Coke Alley toward Washington, New York and Boston."

Someone came up, took a paper, tossed money in the tray, and walked away.

The Paper Man laughed softly.

"I call him Mr. Light with Suit and Tie. Every day he buys a paper. Everyday he pays twenty cents for it instead of twenty five. He thinks he's cheating me."

A woman came by, took a paper, and dropped two quarters in the tray.

"Thank you," the Paper Man said. The woman smiled and hurried on.

"More good folks around, like that nice lady," he said softly. "I call her Nice Lady with Smiling Voice. Her kind more than make up for the Lights."

"Good. Now about the crash house. Any idea where it is?"

The Paper Man chuckled again. "If'n I didn't know where it was, wouldn't have mentioned it. Up in the northeastern section, where Hogg Road crosses Adeline Mail Route. Biggest place on that intersection, which shouldn't be hard for a gent like you to find."

"I'll try," Hawke said. "Anything else on the front burner?"

"Lopez and Hermano. The two boys from south of the border carving up Houston like a big cherry pie. That was the good old days. Now both of them are trying to knock down the other one."

"Who's coming out on top?"

"Lopez has been. Hear his guys hit the Hermano headquarters not an hour ago. You in on that one?"

"Just as an unwilling observer. Paper Man, you take care of yourself now. I got to get back to work."

"Yeah, you better. Lots of work to do in this town. Do one or two of the bastards for me, Avenger. I used to have a brother, he . . . he went down the wrong road and made a pact with the devil weed and the white powder and he ain't . . . he just ain't around no more. You do one or two of them bastards for me."

Hawke reached out his hand and touched the Paper Man's arm.

"I'll shake on that, Paper Man."

Their hands met and gripped, then Hawke turned and walked away toward his van.

He found the intersection in northern Houston after consulting his big map. Houston was no easier, no harder to get around in than any other overcrowded city of two million. He parked halfway down the block on Hogg Street and watched the two-story apartment building on the corner.

Now and then a car entered and left the parking area behind the structure.

A cab pulled up in front of the place and two women got out. Both wore short skirts and tight blouses. One was black, the other a Mexican. They were hookers from the street trade, and they didn't care who knew it. They paid the cabby and walked into the crash house's front door.

The troops must be getting restless.

Hawke rummaged through his clothes until he found the wildest shirt he had brought with him, a bright blue-and-red Hawaiian print that Brandy had bought for him.

He put it on, took the silencer off his .45, and made sure the weapon was hidden under his shirt. He put some socks and underwear in the shoulder ammo bag and tucked three smoke grenades in with them. Then Hawke drove six blocks down on Aldine until he saw some taxi stands and parked. He locked the van and walked up to a cab.

Five minutes later he pulled up in front of the crash house, paid the driver, and got out.

Hawke swaggered as he walked up the front steps and in the door. Nobody was there. A moment later a big Mexican lady stuck her head around a door.

"You staying, too? Damn! Gotta put another chicken in the pot."

A tall, slender black man came around her. He had a .38 in shoulder leather over a white tank-top T-shirt. He frowned.

"Who the fuck you?"

"I meet another damn friendly native. This town is crawling with them. I just got in from the Colombian air run and I'm bushed. They told me their best spot was full so I had to come here. Don't give me no lip or I'll bust you one!"

The black grinned. "Got demoted from a fancy hotel down with us common folks, huh? Damn shame. Fuck it or leave it."

"Nowhere else to stay. Can't risk a hotel. What the hell, you must have a room for me. Mack Wilson is a good enough name. Where can I get off my feet? Been up for thirty-six straight."

"Tough. Who sent you?"

"How the hell do I know? He said come, I come. Lucky the cabby found this hellhole. Where is my room, before I fold up right here on the floor?"

"You sure sound like one of them uppity air men. Hell, back here. Last spot I got. We got food at five-thirty. In here is the dining room. You come here and get it or you go hungry. The entertainment came in a half-hour ago. Two nice ones, look like. You want one of them little asses you get in line."

"I need sleep, man, not ass. Where's the fucking room?"

The house "manager" led him down the hall to a room and pointed. It was fixed up rather well. A bed, easy chair, TV, and a sink and small bath.

On his way down the hall he saw one big room that was set up like an army day room: pool table, big-screen TV, magazines, a rack full of paperback books.

He decided he would hit the place at five-thirty as they were eating. Most of these mules were fringe people. Misguided, running the drugs for a quick buck. Some might not even be sure what they were smuggling. Most were sheep, innocents.

He had three hours to kill.

Hawke went into the pool room. Six men in there looked

at him, then looked away, noncommittal. He watched TV, then, when a pool game was over, took an offered cue and let the black man beat him at eight-ball.

The second game he won, and they got to talking.

"Hear you're on the air run," the black said.

The guy was in his twenties, thin, probably a user.

Hawke nodded, pocketed the fifteen ball. "Yep. Got a week between runs. You have that long?"

"Hell, I'm just a roadrunner. I can take a load any day I want to. Problem is finding me a car. I do the run up to New York. Been on nine missions now without even a traffic stop. I try to do it smart, see.

"Got these Texas cops who think they got a profile on the drug drivers. Hell, yes. They say most of us are black, young, and driving out of the state from two to five A.M. Hell, I foul them up. I got some makeup and look about sixty, no shit. Then I drive during the peak traffic periods getting out of Houston. That messes them up. They can't even see me in the traffic jams. It lasts all the way out of the state, damn near."

Hawke pocketed the thirteen, then missed a combo shot on the ten and eleven.

"You shoot good pool."

"Learn a lot in a stockade," Hawke said, grinning.

"Yeah." The kid missed an easy straight-in, and Hawke cleaned off his stripes and then sank the eight ball. He put up the cue and went over to the paperback books. He found a Western and settled down to read.

The talk was of running "goods" north. Some of them in the place worked the Brownsville route, but most headed north. Drugs up the pike, cash back down.

"Hear they got a skirt driving goods north," one man said.

"Yeah, a Latino who takes her baby with her. Best cover

anybody ever figured. She's made more than a dozen runs. Not a sniff by the Mounties."

"Bitchin'," Hawke said.

"The stuff upstairs any good?" a thin Mexican man asked.

"What stuff?" someone asked.

"The pussy, a black and a Latino."

"Looked good to me."

"Hell, Domingo, any hole with hair around it looks good to you."

"I'm checking it out," the thin Mexican man said, and headed for the door.

"Wear two rubbers, man, one might have a hole in it," someone shouted, and everyone cheered.

Hawke had found out what he wanted to know. These were not the hard cases, not the rotten core of the drugger problem.

They could live.

Damn, was he playing God here? Yes. Judge, Jury and Executioner. He'd taken on all three roles the first time he wiped out a drugger in that fourth-floor room in San Diego. He was committed. There was no going back now.

Who was he to play God?

He was the only one around for the job. It was a job that had to be filled. The American Way was being trampled on by the druggers. Some people said it was a Communist plot to undermine the U.S., but that was ridiculous. It was pure greed by the drug suppliers, wholesalers, and pushers.

The American profit motive was part of the problem, but any good idea can be distorted and misused. That was his real job, to wipe out the profiteers, to dig out the suppliers, and dry up the supply. Without a supply the market would dissolve.

Hawke dropped on the bed in his room. It was comfortable. Lopez supplied his people with a good crash house. He wanted to go to sleep. He'd been up all night on the golf course and then waiting for Diego.

There wasn't time. It was nearly five. In a half-hour everyone would be down to dinner. He checked the WP grenades in his bag. There were three of them, but two would be enough. One he would set in an upstairs room, and the other one in his room. Then he'd fade away and let the crash house burn to the ground.

There would be plenty of small bundles of drugs around to give the police the right idea about the place.

He dozed a moment, then came up suddenly, and checked his watch. It was one he had paid two dollars for. Use a watch until it stopped or malfunctioned and throw it away! He still had a hard time understanding that thinking. He had worked for almost a week mowing lawns when he was a kid to earn enough to buy his first watch.

Just after five-thirty. Now was the time. He held one of the WP grenades in his hand, hiding it against his side as he went out his door and up the steps to the second floor. He saw no one. Down the hall he heard some shrieks and wails of a sexual encounter. He went to the middle room on the other side and tried the door. Open.

Empty. He pulled the safety pin, flipped the WP grenade on the bedding, saw the arming handle pop off, and then he closed the door and hurried downstairs. He triggered the second grenade on the bed in his room and stepped into the hall before the four second fuse train exploded the furiously burning white phosphorous all over the small room.

Hawke walked out the front door without seeing anyone. Someone called to him just as the door closed but he kept on going. At the sidewalk, he turned away from the building and in the direction of where he had left his van.

When he was a block away, he looked back. He could see

smoke coming from the street window on the first floor. That would be his room. He looked back again another block away and saw that there were people standing outside.

A fire siren wailed as a truck raced past him heading for the structure. They were responding too quickly. A good fire crew might save the building. At least it would give the cops a chance to check over the whole place. They should find enough dope to bust a lot of people and close down the crash house.

A small victory.

For a moment a cold chill hit Hawke and he stopped and looked around casually. He saw nothing unusual, nothing threatening.

It had been the same kind of feeling that came all too often in 'Nam, when somebody had a rifle sighting in on him out in the jungle or in the tall grass. He shook off the feeling. This wasn't 'Nam. He continued on to his van, four more blocks.

It was about time he made his attack on the Presidio. He'd find Diego and learn more about the kid's secret entrance. If it wasn't practical, he'd have to use a disguise or something to get as close as possible, then make an all-out assault. That could get dangerous to his health.

Hawke shrugged. The chance to get Lopez was worth it!

CHAPTER SIXTEEN

Hawke continued his walk to the van. Once more he checked behind him, but the way seemed clear. He got in the van and sat there a moment. He had to find Diego before he began his assault on Lopez's castle, the Presidio. There had been enough weakening, softening up. Now was the time.

His mind made up, Hawke pulled the van into the street and headed back toward Carmelita's apartment, where Diego was living. Hawke soon found the North Freeway, Interstate 45, and headed south. He was about a mile into the high-speed roadway when a older blue Chevy pulled up beside him on the driver's side. The rig had its window down on the passenger side and, without any warning, the driver pulled up a small handgun and fired.

Hawke had seen the rig come up, become alert instantly when it did not power on past. He had glanced that way just in time to see the hand come up with a gun.

Hawke slammed his head and torso to the left, hugging the bucket seats, his left hand still holding the wheel, keeping the van moving ahead in what he hoped was a straight line. He let off the gas at once.

This happened in less than a second, and three shots crashed through the driver's side window, shattering a thousand shards of glass over Hawke. The glass granulated into harmless little squares and rectangles.

The slugs went over his head and into the far window, blasting it outward.

Hawke's van had slowed and the Chevy darted past. Before the other driver could recover, Hawke sat up, hit the gas pedal, and twisted the wheel to put his van directly behind the blue Chevy.

Hawke punched the gas pedal again and the van jolted forward, grazing the bumper of the Chevy before the driver got it moving ahead faster.

Then it was a flat-out chase. The Chevy was three or four years old, and not in the best shape. There wasn't a chance it could outrun the year-old Dodge van. Hawke crowded the Chevy's bumper and saw the guy aim his pistol out the left rear window. When the gunman couldn't get a clear shot at Hawke, he lowered the gun.

The Chevy driver cut through the light inbound traffic and narrowly missed getting sideswiped, skidded onto the off-ramp, and charged into the suburban developments.

Hawke let the driver get his Chevy off the freeway, and then closed in on him. He held the .45 out the window with his left hand and pumped four slugs at the Chevy's left rear tire. The third one connected. The Chevy slowed suddenly and Hawke had to come down hard on the brakes to avoid the blue paint.

The Chevy wheeled to the curb and stopped. Hawke was right behind him. He dove across the front seat and slid out the passenger's side door, dropped to the pavement, and looked under the Chevy. A pair of skinny black ankles showed, in running shoes and no socks. Hawke snapped a shot at the legs, missed, and they vanished across the road.

Hawke gunned around the Chevy in pursuit. They were in a lightly built-up area, with blocks of houses alternating with twenty-acre fields not yet developed.

Hawke saw that his attacker was a tall, slender black man, wearing a sport shirt. He could be the same one from the crash house.

As he ran forward, the man snapped a shot at Hawke. The black jumped a ditch and raced into the field. Then in an eye-blink he vanished.

Hawke dropped to his knees. He was in waist-high grass of some kind. Not the ten-foot variety of 'Nam, but plenty high enough to hide a man crawling through it.

Hawke stayed perfectly still and held his breath, but he could hear no movement.

He stood up and charged twenty yards toward the last spot he had seen the man, then dropped out of sight. There had been no shot at him. Hawke listened again.

This time he heard movement to his left. He worked his way that direction through the grass, making the tops of the grass dance and wave. Now he pulled the silencer from his shoulder leather and screwed it on the big .45.

He stood and looked in the direction of the noises he had heard. The tops of the grass waved without any wind. Hawke put three silenced rounds into the area and charged through the grass in a crouch to make a smaller target.

He dropped into cover again as he reached the spot and found his quarry gone.

Listening again, he heard movement to the right. The bastard was zigzagging. Hawke stood and watched the grass move. This time he took large steps in the same direction. He could walk faster than the black could crawl.

He came within eight feet of the grass movement and powered four more rounds into the grass.

There was a quick laugh from the black, who stood near the spot but to the side.

"Been waiting for that. Eight rounds, and no time to load." The black man lifted his .38. "Me, I had time to reload. Lopez say your head is worth a hundred thousand dollars. It's mine." He lifted the .38 to aim it when Hawke fired again, this time from his waist.

The heavy slug rammed through the black's right shoulder, stripping the .38 out of his right hand.

"Bastard!" the man screamed. "You didn't have time to reload that .45!"

The man fell into the grass and Hawke came up and stood over him.

"Didn't need to reload, asshole. Haven't you ever heard of a fourteen-round magazine for the 1911 A-1 Autoloader?"

Hawke picked up the .38 and pushed it in his belt.

"So Lopez put a price on my head and you thought you could collect?"

"Damn near did. Should have had you."

"Should have will buy you a hot seat in hell."

"Probably. You burn down the crash house, right?"

"Got it started. Little present for Lopez. You won't be managing the place anymore."

"It's probably gutted. I yelled at you as you left. I remembered the picture they gave us of you, but I couldn't find it. When I did, you were leaving."

"Lucky me. Unlucky you."

"Doubt if you're in any rush to get me to a doctor or a hospital. Christ! I'm bleeding to death!"

"Tough shit. Little boys shouldn't play with guns."

"I could trade you . . . a ride to the hospital for some information. Something you probably will want real bad."

"Might, if it's about Lopez and his operation."

"Damn right there. This afternoon Lopez is going to try to snuff Hermano and his top two men."

"That's not news. He tries that every week or so."

"It's how he's going to do it."

"What have you got to lose? Keep talking."

"The three of them are taking a trip this afternoon."

"So."

"Flying to Washington D.C. on Western this afternoon. They leave sometime after four. Each of them will have two suitcases full of coke, more than three hundred pounds. More than three million on the street!"

Hawke shook his head. "I don't follow you. Is Lopez going to blast the trio in the airport waiting room with submachine guns or something?"

"No. He's going to blow the plane apart while it's in the air!"

"Lots of people will be on that flight."

"That's the point."

Hawke snapped his look up and nailed the man.

"You jiving me?"

"Hell, no! I was at the Presidio this morning and heard them making final plans. Lopez'll put a suitcase on board with a bomb in it. A timer will be set to detonate the bomb an hour after take-off time. The passenger checking it in won't get on the plane and . . ."

Hawke turned and started running for his van.

"Hey! What about me?" the black man yelled.

"You're bought and paid for. Drive yourself to the hospital!"

Hawke pushed the .45 into his belt holster so it was covered by his shirt and ran away from the wounded man at a right angle to the direction he had come into the field. He made it to the backyard fences and followed them to the street.

A Houston Police car had parked in the edge of the field and an officer walked partway into the grass. He could not see the black man from his position. He noticed Hawke and waved at him.

Hawke waved back and kept walking toward his van. The police car was fifty yards away. The cop evidently had been called by someone in the housing development, or had spotted the chase on the freeway.

Hawke heard the cop shout at him just as he slid into his van and raced down the street. The Houston officer jumped in his prowl wagon and gave chase. Hawke tore through the residential streets as fast as he could, but he was careful not to raise the ire of any locals who might call another cop.

After several miles of driving he figured he had lost the officer, but there could be a radio call out on the van. The cop hadn't been close enough to see the license plate. Would they stop all of the Dodge vans this color in Houston?

Hawke found Interstate 45 and turned south. He had to get to the airport and stop that flight to D.C.! Western. He had arrived on Western, and it had landed at Hobby Airport to the south of Houston. It wasn't far off 45, but it would take a half-hour to get there. He pushed down on the pedal and watched for traffic officers.

His watch showed that it was after three o'clock. Not one hell of a lot of time to get a flight searched and stopped. He could use a bomb scare phone call. That might help save time. He cut off the freeway at the next off-ramp and skidded to a stop at a filling station.

He might have time, he just might. They would have to get the dope-sniffing dogs into action, too. Western could have three or four flights leaving for D.C. after four o'clock. There could be almost three hundred people on that flight! He had to get it stopped! Whichever one it was!

CHAPTER SEVENTEEN

Hawke waited impatiently for the ringing phone to be picked up. At last a voice answered.

"Good afternoon, thank you for calling Western."

"Get me the airport security office at once, this is an emergency!"

"I beg your pardon."

"I want security! There's a bomb on board one of the Western planes. Get me security at once!"

"Yes . . . yes sir!"

He had to talk to a secretary at security before he got someone in authority.

"I can say this just once, so listen closely. There's a drug war on. One big drug king is fighting another one. One drugger is flying to Washington on Western after four this afternoon. He's taking three-hundred pounds of pure cocaine with him. The other big drug supplier in town plans to put a piece of checked luggage on the same plane with a time bomb in it set to go off an hour after departure time.

"I don't know the flight number. Get out your drug-sniffing dogs and bomb-sniffing dogs. Western flights to Washington, D.C.—check them all!"

Hawke hung up and ran back to his van. He hoped things would start moving at Hobby Airport.

It took him another twenty minutes to get there. He parked in a no-parking zone and rushed into the airport. At the end of a corridor he found the area for the security people. He pushed open the door, walked past two more doors, and saw a man come out in uniform.

He nodded, and Hawke went in the door he had come out. Locker room. Three minutes later he had picked a lock and was dressing in uniform-type pants and an Ike jacket that said AIRPORT SECURITY. He ran out the door and followed a corridor down to the flight line.

He saw no special activity. The Western gate was on down the line. He walked quickly, and saw two security men at the gate. One of them had a dog.

A Western plane was just unloading passengers.

"This the one?" Hawke asked as he walked up.

The security man looked at him curiously.

"They dug out all the hands for this one. Is this the plane that will go back to Washington after four?"

"Yeah. Hey, you know anything about these dogs? I never used one before."

"This one for dope or explosives?"

"Dope. The other dog isn't here," the other security man said. "They sent for him."

"Yeah, I used to work dope dogs in San Diego. Better to work the baggage trains. Where do they load on the Western bags?"

"Show you," the first man said, as he gave the leash to Hawke. It was firmly attached to a body harness on the

German shepherd that looked like it weighed about a hundred pounds.

"Sorry, don't know your name," the other man said. He held out his hand. "I'm Carrington."

"Mitchell, Matt Mitchell," Hawke said. "How many possibles we got on this thing?"

"Four; one at four-thirty, one at five, and two at six by different routes. Damn! I wonder if this is a prank?"

"No damn prank from what I heard. Druggers don't care who they kill if they get their man."

"Yeah. Tell me about it. I used to be a narc in Miami."

They came to the lower-level baggage loading area. Long trains of baggage cars were lined up along an endless belt. The baggage handlers picked off the color tags they needed for certain destinations and flights.

Hawke began working the dog along the string of half-loaded cars. Hawke had had basic training in dogs in the DEA and had used drug sniffers before. The basic idea was to give them a long leash and let them work at their own speed.

The dog worked the length of the Western train and sat down beside Hawke.

"So what now?" Carrington asked. "Looks like your woof-woof struck out."

"No way; there just isn't any dope in any of those bags or else it's hermetically sealed and no odor at all can come out. Now we wait for more bags to come down. What flight are these bags to go on?"

"Flight 163. That leaves at three forty-five, about fifteen minutes from now if it's on time. This probably will slow things down."

"We only have one sniffer?"

"Just one on duty now for drugs. The other one is back in training."

"Our luck," Hawke said. The dog pulled at the leash and Hawke let him have his head. He jumped on a bag on the belt going by and began growling and biting at the handle.

Hawke pulled the bag off the belt.

"You better get somebody else down here to open this bag. I think we just picked up some illegal substances," Hawke said.

"Hey, that bag isn't even going on Western," the other security man said.

He went to a house phone and came back.

"Captain himself is coming down."

"Good. What about the crew's baggage? Who inspects it?"

"Nobody, they walk it on themselves."

"Convenient, isn't it? What's this dog's name?"

"Duke, he's Duke."

"Duke and I are going to have a look at the crew's bags on that Western back there we just left. I'll be back in time to check all the Western bags going out after four."

Hawke hurried away from the suspect bag. He couldn't stay and be seen by the captain of security. He was probably the top man, who would know very well that Hawke wasn't a regular security guard.

Hawke went back to the Western plane and up the steps to the plane-level telescoping gate. The flight crew was just coming along the ramp.

"Like Duke here to check your personal baggage," Hawke said with an official voice. "You've heard of the problem."

The flight captain growled a little but put his bag down and let the dog walk around it. The rest of the crew did the same and Duke didn't raise an eyebrow.

"Thanks, we're just trying to keep you people alive all the way to your next destination."

One of the woman flight attendants looked at Duke.

"I love dogs, can I pet him?"

"Not unless you want to complete the flight with only one hand," Hawke said. He turned and took Duke back down the steps to the pavement.

Back in the luggage-loading area, a new train was in. This one was for flight 405, which was set to leave at four-thirty. Already there were a hundred bags on the cars of the little train. Hawke took the leash off Duke and he jumped into each car, sniffing at each bag, moving on, sniffing again.

They worked the eight cars and then Duke sat obediently beside Hawke's left heel, facing forward. Hawke snapped on the leash, praised him, and rubbed his ears.

Carrington hurried up.

"Man, you missed all the fun. The captain opened the case. It was locked so he broke the lock. It had about a kilo of pot in it. We fixed the bag up and took it out to the counter and paged the owner. He came, and the desk man said he was sorry but some bags had been damaged on the equipment, they thought one of them was his, and would he identify it.

"Damn, he flew into a rage. Identified his bag and said the airline owed him a new one. Captain Kennedy stormed up and cuffed the guy before he could more than spit and told him he was under arrest for narcotics violations. The guy damn near shit his pants! He's halfway to the slammer by now."

"Oh, captain says after this little emergency is over, he wants to see you in his office. Didn't say why."

More luggage came down the belt now. Duke stood at the far end of the Western train, sniffed every bag on the belt, and found nothing for fifteen minutes. The word was given that the baggage was all accounted for on flight 405, and it had to be loaded.

"One down," Hawke said. "Not a chance that Duke could miss three hundred pounds of coke in those bags. You saw what he did when he sniffed out that kilo of pot."

Carrington nodded. Men along the line began pulling bags off the belt and stacking them in front of where the next Western train would come in.

It came whipping in, and Hawke led the big dog up to the first car, where he went to work again.

This was flight 182, a direct, nonstop for Washington, D.C. set to take off at five o'clock.

At four thirty-two Duke seemed interested in a bag, then ignored it. Three minutes later he barked and pawed at an expensive leather bag, which was pulled off the line at once. He barked at it until Hawke got him led away and calmed down. He was supposed to get a treat for finding the dope, but Hawke had nothing. He praised the dog and put him back to work.

This time there was no avoiding the captain of security. He came storming in, opened the bag, and found twenty pounds of pure cocaine.

"Looks like we got this one wrapped. This is the flight. Now where the hell is the other dog?"

About that time a pickup came scooting into the area just outside of baggage-loading, and a golden retriever with his handler came out on the run.

"Joe, damn glad you could take time off your golf game and come to work. This must be the plane. Go over every piece of luggage for explosives. Got to be a bomb on here somewhere, we just don't know where."

"Let's hope not," Joe said. "I rolled the bomb squad from city and they are bringing their bomb basket." Joe put the golden to work at the other end of the train.

Hawke kept working the drug dog until the captain tapped him on the shoulder.

"Mitchell, need to talk to you," the man said. He was large and heavy, and had that military stance that said twenty-five years in the MP's before he retired.

He led Hawke to one side. "I'm Captain Kennedy, and this is my outfit. I'm just curious as hell how you got the uniform and what you're doing. You aren't one of my security people."

Hawke snorted. "Hell, no. I'm DEA undercover, and I've been on this guy's ass for two years. I don't want anybody to blow it. When I got here, Carrington was shit-scared. Said he'd never worked a sniffer before. Don't you train your people? We found one chunk of the shit, but not three hundred pounds. There's got to be more."

"DEA. Easy to check. I know Charlie. After this is over we have to have one long talk about cooperation. Now keep Duke working. He could be saving our asses out here today."

Hawke put Duke back in action, but no more cocaine showed up in the luggage. Captain Kennedy had the man who owned the suitcase with the coke in it jerked off the flight, arrested, and sent to county jail.

Hawke watched the other dog. It could find no explosives in any of the bags. They held the bags as long as they could. At ten minutes past flight time, Captain Kennedy released the baggage and it was loaded.

The next plane was due out at six. Captain Kennedy paced the baggage-loading area.

"Damn, thought we had him," Kennedy said. "That was just some freelancer trying to get rich. No three hundred pounds of smack and no bomb in a suitcase. Two flights to go. Christ! There goes the anniversary party. The wife will kill me."

Hawke worked the dog as a new row of baggage came down the line. Most of it went to Western here, so Hawke had the dog working next to the belt. Duke sniffed each bag and box, now and then ran along with one to doublecheck, then worked back.

Hawke began to think what he would do to go around the dog. Some extraordinary procedure. He had seen an occasional bag brought in late and tossed on a baggage train just as it was pulling out. Late arrival, somebody said. Catch the train *after it left the shed* on its way to the plane. Yes! But when and where?

The golden retriever was in the baggage area pickup, not wasting her nose until it was time to work the right bags this time. Hawke kept inventing various schemes in his mind. By this time Lopez would have heard about the explosives check, and the drug sniffer. How did he hope to win? How could Hermano get his six bags on board?

Hawke watched Duke checking the suitcases. There certainly were more soft bags now than ever before. People seemed to prefer them.

Air Freight! There would be no check there. The coke could be sent in three or four containers marked electronic components, or whatever, and no drug sniffer would have access to them, he was sure. How, then, could Lopez get the explosives bag on board?

Late arrival! Hawke asked Carrington to work the dog. He showed him how to handle the dog, and told him that if Duke found something the whole place would know it.

Hawke checked his watch. The bags would be loaded in another five minutes. The air freight must already be on board. The bomb would arrive shortly, but on which plane? Hawke couldn't tell.

Maybe it had gone through before the explosive-sniffer dog had begun working? It was possible, but Hawke figured otherwise. Lopez couldn't take the chance. The dog was here and might find his bag. Lopez would put the explosives bag on late. Hawke was sure of it.

Hawke found what he wanted. One of the little "mules," the strong little diesel-powered rigs that pulled the trains of baggage cars. He saw the key was in this one, and he turned it on and let it idle.

Promptly at ten minutes until six, the baggage train headed for Western 186. Duke had worked the trains for both the Western flights. Neither was full. Hawke watched the train go to the plane. He drove the mule out where he could see and followed it a ways. There was no attempt by anyone to put another bag on the train.

He came back and watched the second train, set for flight 192 and due out also at six. It left the baggage loading area at five until six.

Halfway to the gate for flight 192, a pickup sped up to the mule and waved the driver to a stop.

Hawke had gunned his mule into action as soon as he saw the pickup move. The driver jumped out and had just taken a suitcase from the back of the pickup to put on the first car of the train when Hawke slammed the heavy "mule" into the side of the pickup and jolted the driver off his feet.

Hawke ran around the pickup, grabbed the civilian and the bag. A minute or two later he saw a flashing red light and heard a siren as a security pickup slashed up to the scene.

Captain Kennedy jumped out of the pickup cab and brought with him the golden retriever. The dog approached the suitcase slowly, then growled and attacked the bag, chewing at the handle, pawing it, growling again.

Captain Kennedy put cuffs on the civilian.

"Well, I'd say you're in a lot of trouble. Transporting an explosive device, with the intent to load it on an interstate passenger aircraft. I'd say you're in a bitching lot of trouble."

Hawke got back in the mule and backed it away from the battered pickup just as Kennedy turned toward him.

"Hey, where the hell you going?"

Ignoring the shouted question, Hawke pushed the lever into forward, raced around the stalled baggage train, and darted down the taxi strip to where flight 186 had just begun to move out toward its assigned runway.

He passed dangerously close to the front of the airliner and the pilot shook his fist at him.

Hawke gave him a "cut" sign across his throat, but the pilot did not stop. At last, Hawke came directly at the big plane and stopped in its path. The pilot would have to bring the plane to a halt or run into the mule and damage the plane's landing gear. The big plane stopped with less than ten feet to spare.

By that time Captain Kennedy and two more security vehicles had rushed to the spot. Kennedy walked up to Hawke, arms akimbo.

"What the hell? We got the bomb."

"We got one of them, Captain. The bomb sniffer didn't work the flight we found no dope on, right? That suitcase and bomb went through. Get your sniffer up there and check out the luggage in 186. Bet you a month's pay you'll find a bomb that would have blown that flight out of the sky.

"Then take a look in the air-freight section on both these flights. One of them has three hundred pounds of cocaine on board. The dogs never sniff the air freight."

Captain Kennedy ordered flight 186 back to the gate, where he had the dog do her stuff. She found the bomb after ten minutes of frantic action. She knew it was there somewhere, but the handlers couldn't unpile the bags fast enough to suit her.

Flight 192's air freight compartment had the coke, nearly four hundred pounds in six boxes.

Captain Kennedy scratched his head. "How in hell did you figure this one out?" he asked Hawke.

"Lopez wasn't sure which flight Hermano would take. It could have been any one of four. But he had booked on the flight 405, then canceled. He also booked on 186 and 192 under different names.

"Lopez had to cover both planes. He has an inside man here somewhere and he knew that the dogs were working. When he saw that the explosive dog was not working, he quickly had one of his men send through the baggage bomb on 186. Then he covered his bets by having a flunky, who evidently also is an inside man, make a special delivery to flight 192 after the baggage train left the dog inspector."

Captain Kennedy snorted. "He would have killed almost four hundred people to get rid of three men?"

"When the stakes are this high, a few hundred people mean nothing to these animals."

"We still need that talk."

"Captain, I have to report in to my home office in San Diego, and then check with the locals. I'll use a pay phone so it doesn't come out of your budget. How about your office in a half-hour?"

"Mr. Mitchell, that sounds good. Christ, I hate to think what would have happened here today if you hadn't been on board."

Hawke nodded. "See you in about a half-hour." He walked across the blacktop and concrete to a door marked "Employees Only," went inside, and quickly down to the security offices. He picked up his civilian clothes and faded out the door without talking to anyone.

Five minutes later he had left the no-parking spot where

his van had remained and was on the freeway heading back into Houston.

Mr. Kennedy would have a long wait. Couldn't be helped. Hawke had an important date with Diego, to find out in detail how they were getting into the Presidio.

Tonight was the night. He was ready. Lopez would be mad as hell about the airport fiasco. A good time to hit the drugger and give him a short, bitter taste of hell!

CHAPTER EIGHTEEN

Hawke drove slowly past Carmelita's apartment house. He saw no gunmen sitting in cars, noticed no one loitering on the street who might be a threat. By the time he got there the lights were on in other apartments, but no lights showed in Carmelita's apartment.

He parked and waited a half-hour, then he drove away, and checked the bus where the Toros gathered. There were only two of them there, with a pair of candles burning. The boys had not seen Diego.

They both showed a great deal of respect for Hawke. They said that, if Diego came in, they would tell him Hawke wanted to talk to him.

Hawke drove back to the apartment.

Another half-hour later he saw Diego coming up the street. Hawke met him and they walked past the apartment.

"You think it's dangerous to go inside?" Diego asked.

"Could be. Lopez will blame anyone he can for all the

things that are going wrong for him. Any luck finding a job?"

"I'm still looking. The priest helped me find Carm's will. She had an insurance policy I never knew about."

"She thought ahead, that girl did." Hawke hesitated. "You said once you could get me into the Presidio anytime I was ready. Does that offer still hold?"

"Sure. Only you'll be killed in there. Lopez has dozens, maybe fifty, guards and hit men inside his fortress."

"I have a way of dealing with them." They walked along in silence for a ways. "Diego, would this put you in any danger, getting me inside? If it would, forget it."

Diego was quiet for a moment. "That man killed my sister, had her killed. The police told me she had been beaten and tortured, cut and broken and . . . and violated as well. Lopez deserves to die for what he did. I know I wouldn't last for two minutes inside, but you might. You know how to take care of yourself."

They came to the van and Hawke stopped.

"What happened to the windows?"

"A little trouble with the natives."

"Damn sure about that!"

"The cops might even have an ID on it. I'm not sure. I might have you fix it up for me."

"Glass is easy. You still have your goods?"

"A skilled craftsman can never work without his tools. I could use some more, but I probably have enough. Then it's on for tonight?"

Diego laughed softly. He had grown up a lot in the short time Hawke had known him.

"Yes, it's on. I have the easy part. When do we go into the place?"

"No rush. I want to let some of the foot traffic die down

and the foot soldiers get a little weary on their posts. About midnight, probably. You have supper yet?''

''I can always use another cup of coffee.''

They got in the van and Diego guided him to a fast-food eatery that specialized in Southern fried chicken.

As they ate, Diego seemed anxious to talk.

''I've applied at three computer stores. I figure I can learn a lot about computers by selling them, and then when I get into the part about how they work I'll have some background. That should make me more valuable as a salesman, too. I pushed the idea that I'm bilingual, and I think it helped.''

They ate the chicken and dessert and lingered over iced tea and coffee.

''You said you were DEA once. How did you get into that work? You never told me.''

So Hawke went over his career quickly. The service, then the cops and San Diego State at night, the Narco squad and finally the DEA.

''I don't think I'll go into the service. I'll have a job soon, and I can go to Houston Community College the first two years. Then maybe a four-year university or a tech school in computers.''

A half-hour later they went back to the van and talked some more. About eleven, Diego began to fidget.

''Shouldn't we get started?'' Diego asked.

''What's the procedure?''

''We drive up toward the Presidio. About a mile this side of it we park and go for a walk. I'll explain it when we get there.''

When they arrived in the vicinity of the Presidio, Diego showed him where to park. They picked out a spot under a streetlight for added safety for the van.

Hawke opened the storage and took out the equipment he

would need. He had the M-16 and grenade launcher, a shoulder bag for grenades, and 40-mm rounds for the launcher. He put in six thirty-round magazines for the M-16, and four magazines loaded with fourteen rounds for his .45 automatic.

"Man! I've never seen so much fire power!" Diego said.

"Working tools a man needs when he's out skunk-hunting." Hawke added four quarter-round blocks of C-4 plastic explosive, and put pencil-timer detonators in his pocket. He had changed into his black pants and the black jersey with the long sleeves. Over that he wore a camouflage shirt, and a web belt to hold the big .45, with pouches hooked into the eyelets.

In one final move he slipped an inch-wide, blood-red stretch band around his head.

"Now if we can get to the entrance spot before we get bagged by some lucky Houston cop, we'll be okay," Hawke said.

They walked down an alley, and came to a dead end. They had been moving downhill, and at the end of the alley Hawke saw the entry point. Diego sat down on the curb, and quietly removed six steel guards that had been loosened. The steel rods had guarded the opening to the storm drain where runoff water was carried downgrade to an outlet.

Diego sat down and scooted feet-first into the eighteen-inch opening.

"Piece of cake," Diego's voice said from the darkness. "There's a two-foot drop to a six-foot-high drainpipe. You brought the flashlight, didn't you?"

Hawke followed where the young man had led. Once inside, he snapped on a flashlight and gave a second one to Diego.

"Like I told you, this section of the storm drain was by-passed when they closed up a street and made a park.

From here on up the hill it's always dry. Only thing is, we can't make too much noise or somebody might hear us at some of the half-closed-up drain entrances."

They moved quickly then, having to stoop over now and then where silt had built up in the pipe. They saw lights through some of the drain entrances, but there was no wetness.

"You did this before?"

"We used to play dungeons and dragons in here. With water pistols and a hundred variations."

"How far is it?"

"We figured it has to be about a mile. We'll come to some branches. That's when it gets tricky."

"But coming out, I just stick to the downhill slope, right?"

"You don't want me to wait for you?"

"Could be too dangerous. I'll feel better if you're back on top when the shooting starts."

Ten minutes later Diego shone his light on a steel ladder leading upward. His light picked up a set of spraypaint-can graffiti near the ladder.

"This is the place," he whispered. "The ladder leads up to a manhole-type cover, and a sub-basement. The basement is a storage area that isn't used much. We got into it, and looked out a door, and then chickened out. I don't know where it leads after that. But one thing is certain. You'll be right in the basement of the four-story mansion where Alejandro himself lives. The toughest part of the Presidio to get into. In there I've heard they shoot first and explain who the dead man is later."

"I'll damn well be careful. Now get out of here," Hawke said. "I'll either meet you back at the van or at your place. After tonight it should be safe enough. You take the van back, get it off the street."

Diego held out his hand in the flashlight beam.

"Hawke, I want to thank you . . ."

"Hell, kid, I'll see you again. You still have to show me where to catch those big catfish you bragged about. Now get moving."

Diego grinned and walked back down the storm drainpipe.

When Hawke was sure Diego was going, he put his feet on the first rungs of the steel ladder and moved upward. The rungs went up twenty feet, then Hawke felt the plate above him. He hoped nobody had welded it shut. He put his shoulder to it and surged upward.

The heavy iron cover popped up an inch, then another, and soon pivoted to one side. A rush of fresh air hit him. There was little light in the place. He pushed the cover aside more and squeezed through the opening to the solid floor. As quietly as possible he tugged the cover back into place.

His eyes were well adjusted to the darkness. Now, in the soft light filtering in through a half-open door, he saw the surroundings. A storage room, not much used. Quickly he moved to the doorway and peered out. Another room, that had been used more. A wooden stairway led upward.

Hawke screwed the silencer onto the .45 and fisted it as he moved up the steps. The door was cracked open and he looked through it. The room was much like the one he was in, only it had more the look of a weapons storage and powder magazine. Hawke studied it again.

Yes! Weapons, explosives, even a sign-out system, it seemed. Lopez must have a regular army of men working out of here. Hawke checked the protection. One man sat in a chair near the far door. There was a second area in back of a Dutch door where he could see racks of guns. A man moved up to the opening now and then.

He could see no one else in the area. The outside guard had a submachine gun across his lap.

Hawke leveled out the heavy, silenced .45 past the edge of the door, and squeezed off one shot. The big Mexican guard's forehead shuddered as the .45 blasted into it. A huge stain showed behind him on the wall where warm, red blood ran down the wall in streaks. The guard's head slammed against the wall for a moment, then he settled back in the chair in an eternal position.

Hawke stepped into the room, saw the open door, and darted to it. He closed it and pushed a bolt. Then he moved silently to the half-door.

"Hey!" Hawke called in an angry, impatient tone.

"Yeah, yeah, I'm coming." The Anglo came around a rack of weapons. When he saw Hawke his eyes went wide, and he pawed for a .38 at his hip.

Hawke's .45 whispered once more and the inside weapons man died before he could take another step. The back of his head exploded as the .45 round smashed through his skull and into a rack of riot shotguns.

Hawke slipped inside the storage room, found six cases of dynamite and added to them three of the quarter-pound chunks of his C-4 explosive. He set a detonator for thirty minutes, pushed the pencil-sized timer combo into the soft plastic goop, and activated it.

That should make a big bang. Hawke set the timer on his watch that would tick off the time, and came out of the room. He picked up the submachine gun from the dead guard, found a pair of spare magazines and put them in his bag. The chopper went over his shoulder on its sling.

At the hallway door he paused. He pushed the night lock on the door so it would lock when he closed it. Then he jammed a piece of soft copper wire into the keyhole so it would be impossible to open the lock.

Hawke closed the door and unslung the big M-16. He had charged a round into the chamber and now moved ahead with both the .45 and M-16 ready. The big man's office would be on the third or fourth floor. Hawke saw a flight of stairs and went up. He was almost at the top of the steps when a man started down. When he saw Hawke he jerked back and dug for his pistol, but Hawke shot him twice in the chest and pushed him down the steps.

He paused as he came to the door at the second floor. A small man with a moustache and beard came out of a room carrying a tray. Food? For a prisoner?

Hawke grabbed the man from behind, put the silenced .45 against the man's forehead.

"The prisoner. Where is the prisoner?"

The small man shook so hard he nearly dropped thc tray.

"Prisoner, Reno Johnson. Right inside! Don't kill me. I'm just a cook here."

"Open it!" Hawke ordered.

The man fumbled with the keys. Hawke took the tray from him and he got the door open. Hawke pushed him inside and looked in. Reno sat on a chair, tied in place. No one else was in the room.

Hawke stepped in, closed the door, and locked it.

"Hi, Reno. You're a hard man to find."

"Hawke! I'll be damned. Knew those assholes in San Diego read you wrong. You're just undercover, right?"

Hawke used his knife to cut the nylon cord that held Reno in the chair.

"Hell, no, I'm not undercover, Reno. I'm on my own. You don't see any of the local DEA guys rushing in here to bail you out." He paused. "Your wife is fine. Now, stand up and get some circulation back in your legs and arms. We got to get you back in fighting shape for the job coming up."

"Getting out of here?"

"Eventually. First we do a payback on Lopez for a fine

young woman by the name of Carmelita Salazar. You know her. Lopez had her killed."

"Christ, no!"

"Afraid so." Hawke tossed Reno the submachine gun. It was an Ingram Model 10, chambered for 9-mm Parabellum rounds. "Can you use this?"

"Damn right! I owe these bastards, too!" Johnson held up his left hand, displaying the stump of his little finger wrapped in a piece of dirty, bloody rag.

Hawke gave him the extra magazines.

"You know where Alejandro is?" Hawke asked.

"This late, probably in his office suite, top floor."

"How many guards on a floor?"

"Two, maybe three. All have choppers."

"Easy. We're still soft. They don't know we're here yet." Hawke looked at his watch. "We have sixteen, seventeen minutes before the big bang comes. The power magazine is going to blow sky-high."

The small Latino cook had been listening with wide eyes. He shook as he faced the two gunmen.

"Did this one hurt you?" Hawke asked.

"No, no, don't shoot him. He brought me extra food. He's one of the few human ones around here."

"Tie him up to the chair and let's move."

Hawke stepped into the hall a moment later and heard a scream from down a flight. A guard jumped into the corridor thirty feet away and Hawke sprayed him with six rounds from the M-16.

That started the firefight. Hawke and Reno charged down the short way to the stairs. Reno covered his back while Hawke pulled a hand grenade from his bag and jerked the pin out. He started up the steps just as two men opened the door on top and came down.

Hawke let the handle pop on the grenade and held it an

impossibly long two seconds before he flipped it into the air at the two men twenty feet up the steps. Hawke jolted back around the corner just as the hand bomb exploded in midair three feet in front of the two guards. They dissolved their lives in a ripping, tearing, killing shower of shrapnel that nearly tore them apart.

Hawke and Reno surged up the stairs, stepping over the bloody remains of the men, kicking open the door. Hawke saw movement and sent a chatter of eight rounds down the hallway.

They charged on up the stairs, reaching the fourth floor, and when Hawke hit the door with the butt of the M-16, he jerked back quickly. A hail of hot lead tore through the thin door.

Reno returned the fire through the door and heard a long sigh as the noise quieted.

Hawke pushed open the barrier and found a man half cut in two by 9-mm Parabellums just inside the door.

They kicked him aside and headed down the corridor. This one was shorter. Only three doors led off it.

"I was up here once. Lopez has the whole left half of the floor," Reno said.

The whole building shook and they heard a roar from deep in the structure. The lights flickered.

"Greetings," Hawke said. "My sympathy card for the house."

For a moment the building creaked and groaned, but it stood.

Two more guards rushed out of the far door on the right.

Reno and Hawke stood shoulder to shoulder in the hall.

"Right!" Hawke bellowed, and slammed six rounds into the right-hand man. Reno picked up on the signal and did a figure "S" on the second guard on the left at the same time. They both toppled backward without getting off a shot.

The door closest to Hawke and Reno opened during the firing, and before they saw it a handgun came around the molding and fired six shots.

One cut Hawke deep in the right thigh, a second one grazed his shoulder. One of the rounds caught Reno in the shoulder.

"Cover me!" Hawke shouted. He dug in his bag for a fragger, found one, jerked the pin out, and dove forward to get an angle at the open door. He threw the grenade like a baseball, bouncing it off the half-opened door and into the room.

Four point two seconds later the bomb went off, and a high keening sound came from the room for ten seconds, then weakened and ended in a death rattle.

Reno charged in and cleared the room.

"Dead," he said, stepping out after having slammed a dozen rounds into the room as he entered.

Hawke hit the wall beside the door on the left, Lopez' place. The ex-DEA agent hoped the big man was home.

Hawke kicked the door from the side.

Nothing happened.

He kicked it again. There was no response. He aimed the M-16 at the doorknob and lock and drilled six rounds through the mechanism.

Slowly the door opened and swung inward.

"For God's sake, don't shoot anymore!" a heavily accented voice shouted. "I've got two women in here."

"Come out naked with your hands laced on top of your head!" Hawke bellowed.

There was some whispering.

"I'll send the women out. Don't hurt them. Are you this Hawke?"

"Come and see," Hawke said.

The women came out, each wearing a robe. Both were

blonde and young, and frightened. Hawke let them go, then surged into the room at an angle, diving the last step and skidding on his stomach with the M-16 up and ready.

He was in an office with carpet on the floor, a fancy desk, hunting trophies on the wall, and dozens of plaques and pictures.

Lopez was not there.

Hawke lifted up and ran to a connecting door. He kicked it open, but there was no volley of shots. He looked in. It was a bedroom, as big as the twenty-foot-square office. A window stood open, with the curtains blowing inward.

Hawke rushed to it. There was an extension of the third floor under the window. On the far side of the roof, fifty feet away, he saw something move in the darkness.

On the roof, Hawke made out a form. He wasn't sure if it was Lopez or not. Hawke lifted the M-16 but had no target. Then he heard a sound he couldn't recognize. To the left he saw fire break out through some windows. It made enough light to see something he didn't believe.

A man at the edge of the building swung out into space from three stories up!

Then the light brightened and Hawke saw the reason. The man was Lopez, and he held onto two handles attached to a pair of rollers. The device was hanging on a cable! It was a cable slide down to the ground!

Hawke fired at the figure as he sped down the cable into the darkness, but he was gone too quickly.

Reno charged into the room behind Hawke.

"This way!" Hawke shouted. "We can get down one story at a time. Alejandro is down on the ground by now."

They ran across the roof of the third floor and dropped to the second level, then to the first and then they jumped to the ground. Reno twisted his ankle, but he was up at once.

"There's a gate down here, and a strip of lawn. That's probably where Lopez came down."

Behind them the fire on the first floor raged. It seemed everyone was over there fighting the blaze.

Hawke and Reno charged through the gardens, into the grass strip. Ahead they saw a car heading for a gate.

Hawke saw a second car in the parking area. It had keys in it and a sleepy driver in the front seat. Hawke thudded the butt of the M-16 into the man's throat and jerked him out of the car. Reno slid into the passenger's side.

Lopez' car careened around a corner and sped away. Hawke started the engine of the heavy car, a Caddy he thought, shifted it into drive and spun rubber off the tires as he screeched out after the biggest drug dealer in Houston.

"He'll lose us!" Reno shouted.

"Not a chance!" Hawke said. "I didn't drive a taxi in San Diego for the fun of it!" Hawke tromped on the gas and closed the gap between the two big cars.

CHAPTER NINETEEN

Lopez could drive a car! Hawke soon learned that he would have all he could manage just to keep the new black Lincoln in sight. The man knew the town and made the big car do exactly what he wanted it to.

They whipped through several residential streets, slammed down narrow alleys, moved on to a light industrial park and maneuvered in, through and around freight, working night crews on loading platforms, and across one big warehouse.

No one shot. At these speeds and distances the only thing that would have been effective was the M-16, and Reno had begged off on that.

"Hell, I'd probably kill a dozen civilians before I got Lopez," Reno said.

Taking a sharp turn, the Caddy skidded on two wheels, threatening to roll, but the pure weight of the big car kept it upright.

"Lopez can drive," Reno said.

"Where the hell is he heading?" Hawke asked. "You know the town. Where are we? What's ahead?"

"First he was just trying to ditch you. He's up against a driver as good as he is. Now he's moving east into the Magnolia Park district. That's right next to the ship channel. Yeah! I know for damn sure that he has some boats along there. One time we had him tracked as owning more than twenty power boats."

"Can he drive them, too?"

"Damn right. He used to run boats as well. He worked out the system of dropping goods from planes out in the Gulf long before the guys doing it now even thought of it. Had a light on them in watertight containers. I hear that's how he made his first big money."

They screeched around another corner. The traffic on the roads and streets had thinned out, but still there were too many innocents around to do any shooting, Hawke decided.

A few minutes later they hit 75th Street, barreled through traffic, jumped through a red light at Navigation, and boiled into Foster near the public wharves.

"Yeah, he's got a boat here somewhere," Reno said.

"Where can we get a boat?"

"Too late for the tourists, too early for the fishermen. Though we might find somebody at the Port of Houston Harbor Patrol office."

"Where?"

"Half a block down on the right."

"Look, Lopez is dumping his car right there. By the time we get to the Harbor Patrol office, he'll be hidden where we can't find him. Let's try for a boat and watch for him to come out."

Hawke drove back to the black Lincoln Lopez had just left. He saw that the driver's side window was down. From his bag he took a WP grenade, pulled the pin, and dropped the fire bomb in the Lincoln's driver's seat, then charged down the street.

The grenade went off with a pop and spewed burning white phosphorous into the seat, dash, and all over the fancy car. It blazed up in a minute and kept burning—phosphorous is nearly impossible to put out until it burns itself out.

A half-block down Hawke eased to a stop near the Port of Houston boat dock. One patrol boat sat there, running lights on, engine purring softly. Two men talked on the small dock.

Both Hawke and Reno walked down to the dock.

"You ask one of them a question he'll need to go back to the little office for. Then I'll get the boat. Tell him you're DEA and he'll help you."

"Yeah, easy. And you grab the boat?"

"Only way, man. Team effort."

They walked up to the two Harbor Patrol officers.

"Evening. Just thought I should tell you men you've got a car on fire half a block down. We drove past and it was burning like hell!"

One of the officers ran up to the street to look. The other one pointed to the boat.

"Like to help, but Paul will take care of it. I'm due out on patrol."

Hawke shoved the .45 in the officer's gut.

"I'll handle the patrol. Don't make a bad move." He lifted the revolver from the man's holster and jumped on the boat. He cast off the one line holding the twenty-four-foot patrol boat and looked at the controls a minute, then gunned the engine, turned the wheel, and edged away from the dock.

"You won't get half a mile!" the port officer yelled.

Hawke eased farther into the channel and moved out where he could check the series of wharves. Before he figured it would happen, a power boat slammed out of a closed boat house and raced down the channel.

Hawke rammed the throttle forward and charged after the other boat. Hawke had to leave the long gun in the car when he came down to the dock. Now he wished he had it and the grenade launcher.

His boat could match the other for speed. Lopez' craft was a twenty-footer and built for speed. It sent up a rooster tail behind it as it turned slightly and jolted forward.

Hawke matched the other boat's speed for a couple of minutes, then powered across a wide turn the other boat made and closed the range.

He saw a shotgun in a holder near the wheel. When he pulled it he saw the lock. One round from his .45 broke the hasp and he pulled out the long gun. When he checked it he found it was loaded with five rounds of double-ought buck. The thirteen slugs inside the three-and-a-half-inch shell were as big as thirty-two caliber bullets.

Now, he needed to get close enough.

He pushed the throttle forward again and saw the engine gauge move over the red line, but he held it. The engine screamed with the added power and the patrol boat leaped ahead. In twenty seconds he had closed the range to thirty yards. He balanced the shotgun over the plastic windscreen and fired.

Wide. He gunned closer, pumped the weapon and caught Lopez cutting to the side. The shot from the scatter gun drilled a dozen holes in the side of the white ship.

Lopez staggered.

Hawke pumped the gun and aimed and fired again. The rounds blasted the control panel in front of Lopez and pitched him backward. The other boat slowed, and Hawke cut back his own throttle.

A few moments later the engine on Lopez' craft died and

she went dead in the water. Hawke brought his boat up close and cut the engines. At six feet he blasted a round across the deck. The last round in the shotgun he put in at the water line, and saw the craft begin to take on water.

Hawke fisted his .45 and waited.

He drifted away from the smaller boat, then gunned the engine to come around, and as he did he saw a man fall into the water from the side of the boat.

In the darkness, Hawke edged closer. The power boat was sinking. In another five minutes it would be on the bottom.

He searched the water. A form, a black blob, swam slowly toward the shore fifty feet away. Hawke powered toward the swimmer.

Hawke put two .45 slugs into the water beside the man.

Lopez stopped swimming and turned to face Hawke.

"Bastard!" he screamed. "You blow up my house. You kill my people! And for what?"

"Because you're scum and shouldn't be allowed to breathe the earth's free air. You kill a hundred thousand people a year with your heroin, pot and cocaine. If I can stop you from hooking just one kid in grade school, I'll be happy."

"You're an idiot!" Lopez had been treading water. He turned over on his back and floated.

"You're a dead man, Lopez. You die once for killing Carmelita Salazar. You die once for each kid and man and woman you've pushed down with you into drugs."

"I'm not dead yet, bastard!"

"You will be soon. Shooting is too good for you. You deserve something slow and painful, like bleeding to death, or drowning."

Hawke pushed the throttle forward so the patrol boat moved slowly through the water. He tied down the wheel after pointing the craft toward the shore, then dove off the boat. He surfaced six feet from Lopez.

"I'm wounded!" Lopez screamed. "Get me to a doctor."

"You don't get a doctor, Alejandro," Hawke said. He swam toward him, then behind him, and grabbed him from behind as if in a lifesaving carry.

Then Hawke pushed the drug king's head under the water, held it for ten seconds, and let it come up. Lopez sputtered and screamed.

"Think about dying, Lopez. You're probably a Catholic. Think about eternity in the fires of hell!" Hawke pushed his head down again. This time the drug king struggled less. A few bubbles came up.

Hawke let him pop up. He struggled, trying to get his hands on Hawke.

"Remember all the innocent men you have killed, you drug terrorist. Think of all the sour deals where you and your men came out shooting. Think about all the good cops you wasted!"

Hawke pushed Lopez' head down again and this time kept it there. When the man stopped struggling, Hawke left his head under water for another two minutes. When he let go of Lopez, his body sank for a moment, then lifted and drifted slowly down the channel.

Hawke swam to the far side of the channel. The power boat had stuck on shore as he hoped it would. He climbed in, used the screw to pull it off the small mud bank, and worked back up the channel until he found a dock. He came in and tied the craft to the dock, then hurried away from it. Far up the channel he heard a siren. He figured it was another patrol craft. Their little boat wasn't hurt. They were out only five shotgun shells and some dignity.

Hawke decided he better make some time to get away from the area. The Port Police would throw out a dragnet to try to find him. Maybe he could hitch a ride.

* * *

Two days later, Hawke and Diego fished from the shore about five miles down from where Hawke had left the ship channel.

"I got the job in the computer store," Diego told him. "I start tomorrow. Grunge work, but I have a chance to learn and move up."

"Good. The services for Carmelita were beautiful."

"It was the way she wanted it. How did she know she might not live long?"

"From her days as a cop. All cops make out their wills, or at least they should."

"She had that insurance policy. I didn't want to take the money. What can I do with twenty thousand dollars? The agent worked out a deal where I get two hundred a month for fifteen or sixteen years, depending on interest rates. That means I can go to school full-time. I worked it out with the store."

"I'm sure she is pleased with the arrangement."

"Hey, hey! Look at your line!"

Hawke pulled up sharply, hooked the creature on the other end, and soon had a two-pound catfish dangling from his line.

"These things are good to eat?" Hawke asked.

"Yeah, and Carm taught me how to cook them."

"Deal. This enough for both of us?"

"Plenty."

"Then let's roll. I have a plane to catch."

"You said you talked to somebody in San Diego?"

"Right, Brandy. She's got all my DEA files on computer and she keeps me posted on the latest drugger news. She says there's a big drug war going on in Miami that I need to cover. Maybe I can help drive up the cost of doing business there. Miami and on to Colombia. Why not cut off the supply before it hits our coast? Colombia is where most of our coke comes from. I really need to get to the heart of the problem.''

''You need any help?''

''How many men have you killed lately?''

''Not a whole lot.''

''Diego, the help I want from you will come in getting my own computer set up right so I can tap into the federal memory banks, the DEA, the FBI, and some local operations like the Miami Narc Squad.''

Diego grinned. ''I'm not a hacker, but I'll learn.''

Hawke laughed and headed for the Dodge camper van. Diego would turn it in for him and pay for the damage with money Hawke gave him. Hawke's weapons were at the bottom of the ship channel, except for his silenced .45, which would go deep in his checked baggage.

He looked forward to Miami. That was where eighty percent of all the cocaine smuggled into the United States made its entry. Where there were so many boats and planes heading inland that the authorities simply had to pick which one to stop and let the others go.

He had to find and nail the drug kings, the imports. Melt down a billion in coke and he'd have a start on Miami.

He had packaged most of the captured two million dollars in cash in a sturdy cardboard box, and sent it by first-class mail to Brandy at their apartment in San Diego. She would deposit it nine thousand at a time in their accounts. First he had taken out two hundred thousand to take with him for spending money. He might have to buy a boat or a plane to get where he wanted to go next. The money was all in hundreds, and kept in a slender attaché case.

Hawke nodded at Diego.

''Let's get this show on the road,'' he said. As they drove away he thought, ''For you, Connie. Everything I do now is in your memory. Every time I nail another one of these drugger bastards ruining our children, wasting our adults, I'm doing it in your memory. Goodbye, Connie, my best friend. Goodbye, Connie, my wife. Rest in peace."

At the Houston airport Hawke reviewed the Miami contacts he had developed while working with the DEA there. Nofrando would be his first Miami contact. He was just high enough in the drug trade to know both sides.

Hawke slammed his fist into his hand, startling the man beside him in the ticket line. He was moving again, ready. He was The Avenger, and he was anxious to get to Miami to get started.

A New Western adventure series from Warner Books ! ! !

__HELLBREAK COUNTRY (C30-621, $2.75, U.S.A.)
Jackson Cain (C32-079, $3.50, Canada)
Gritty realism, spicy sex, and meticulously researched, authentic historical detail. Ride the hellbreak trail with the orneriest outlaw in the Old West, Torn Slater, and his willing women.

__SAVAGE BLOOD (C30-622, $2.75, U.S.A.)
Jackson Cain (C32-224, $3.50, Canada)
Torn Slater returns with the most notorious folks of his time: Wild Bill Hickok, General Custer, Calamity Jane, Geronimo, Frank and Jesse James, and others.

__HANGMAN'S WHIP (C30-623, $2.75, U.S.A.)
Jackson Cain (C32-346, $3.50, Canada)
The third in this blazing, hot-blooded Western adventure series. Many men have tried to stop Torn Slater. They are all dead now. A crazy crapshoot with death is just the kind of game Slater plays best.

WARNER BOOKS
P.O. Box 690
New York, N.Y. 10019

Please send me the books I have checked. I enclose a check or money order (not cash), plus 50¢ per order and 50¢ per copy to cover postage and handling.* (Allow 4 weeks for delivery.)

_______ Please send me your free mail order catalog. (If ordering only the catalog, include a large self-addressed, stamped envelope.)

Name ______________________________

Address ______________________________

City ______________________________

State ____________________ Zip __________

*N.Y. State and California residents add applicable sales tax.